Whodunit Award Runner Up 2018

Homicide
in the
Headlines

Mark Zeid

ABSOLUTELY AMAZING eBOOKS

ABSOLUTELY AMAZING eBOOKS

Published by Whiz Bang LLC, 926 Truman Avenue, Key West, Florida 33040, USA.

For information contact:
Publisher@AbsolutelyAmazingEbooks.com

ISBN-13: 978-1949504255 (Absolutely Amazing Ebooks)
ISBN-10: 1949504255

Homicide in the Headlines

Chapter One

Terry groaned as he reached for the phone ringing on his desk. Someone with a sick sense of humor had put it out of his reach. He climbed on top of his desk and pulled the phone to him before sitting back down. He cursed himself as he knocked over a photograph of a pretty brunette. "Sorry about that," Terry said to the photograph as he set it upright. He picked up the receiver for the phone. "Hello," he said trying to get comfortable in his specially-made chair, "*City Times*, copy editing. How can I help you?"

"I'm helping you," a voice distorted by a machine replied. Terry listened as the person chuckled at the other end.

Terry took a deep breath. "Well I certainly appreciate that. How are you going to help me?"

"I've got a killer of a story," the distorted voice said while laughing.

"Excellent. We are always looking for good stories. What's this one about?"

"No, no, no," the voice said in a taunting manner. "You have to work for it."

"Okay," Terry said drawing out the word. "And how am I going to do that?"

"There's an abandon shopping center on Highway 41. Look around back. You'll find your story." The voice hung up.

Terry looked at the handset before setting it back on phone. He sat there, thinking how to handle the situation.

"Hey, didn't I see you with Snow White?"

Terry groaned again; another voice he didn't want to deal with. This one belonged to Ashford Zane, one of the paper's top reporters and probably the practical joker who put Terry's phone out of his reach. However, as far as Terry was concerned, Ashford was as welcomed as a hemorrhoid, a real pain in the ass.

"Now, which one are you," Ashford said chuckling at his joke. "Is it Grumpy, Sleepy, Doc, Dopey, which one."

Terry looked up at Ashford. "I'm the one who doesn't like jokes about dwarfs. And I don't like it when you put my phone at the edge of my desk so I can't reach it, and then call me about some bogus news story, just so you can watch me struggle answering the phone."

"Hey, I didn't call you about a bogus story, although I would have if I thought of it. Also, it's not my fault you're only four feet tall."

"Well it isn't my fault either. It's not like I choose it on my college application."

"Listen half pint. Don't give me any crap."

Terry glared at Ashford. "Just leave the stuff on my desk alone."

"Yeah, sure," Ashford said as he walked past Terry, pressing Terry and his chair into the editor's desk.

"Ashford," called out a feminine voice. "Quit picking on Terry."

Ashford turned to face the woman. "Diana. Come on. I'm just joking around with the runt. I'm not going to hurt him."

Diana stood with her arms crossed. "Sometimes your jokes aren't funny. Besides that, no one really appreciates your practical jokes; especially the one last week with the dead rattlesnake in women's toilet."

"Aw come on, that was funny. You should have seen you girls running out of there."

"The snake was probably one of your relatives," Terry

mumbled to himself.

"You say something," Ashford said challenging Terry.

"Yeah," Terry replied. "If you didn't call me, then who did? I got a strange phone call. Someone said there was a story behind the abandon shopping plaza on Highway 41."

"What else did the caller say?" asked Diana.

"Nothing really," Terry answered. "He just said there was a killer of a story out there. I thought it was Ashford and one of his practical jokes the way the guy was laughing."

"Probably was a prank." Ashford replied. "It's not worth running out there. If there is a story, someone will call it in."

"I don't know," Terry said. "If it isn't a prank, then someone should check it out."

"Ashford's right," Diana added. "It there is a news story, others will call it in. People are more likely to call the media about a crime or incident than they are to call the police."

"Do you really think people are that sick?" Terry asked.

"Yeah, they are," was Ashford's response.

~ ~ ~

He giggled as he removed the sim card from the disposable phone. He made a mental note to throw them both away, possibly in the river near the railroad tracks. He wasn't worried about anyone tracing the call, but if the police found the phone, they might be able to trace it back to where he bought it and when. He didn't want to show up on any video recordings. He called a newspaper and it was the first time, so he knew they wouldn't have any equipment set up for tracing phone calls. The police would go through phone records. They would find the number and probably be able to triangulate the signal to this area, which wasn't a problem. He wanted them to find this place. How else would they find the dead girl's body?

~ ~ ~

Woody Dumfries loved the interesting people he met while driving a taxi. Sure, there were some who gave him hassles; but as a retired boxer and a very large black man, Woody had no trouble getting those who stepped out of line to mind their manners. Twice, someone had tried to rob him. Both times, Woody gave them the money, let them out of the cab, called the police, then chased the thieves down himself. He admits he was lucky. The first time the thief ran down an alley and Woody followed him in the taxi, knocking the thief down with the driver's door. The second time the thief ran into a building and started up the stairs; but he slipped, fell down, and dropped the gun. He got up and took a swing at Woody, who immediately decked the thief, knocking him out cold. Still, Woody had learned to be careful and made it a point to check out fares before they got into his cab. He noticed a small man hailing a cab.

Woody pulled his taxi over to the curb. The short man jumped in. "Where to?" Woody asked.

"Pardon?"

"Where do you want to go?"

"Oh. Yeah. Ah, I need to go to an abandon shopping center on Highway 41."

"The one across the highway from the museum?"

"I guess," Terry answered. "All I know is some guy called and said there was a big story and it was behind an abandon shopping center on Highway 41."

"Is that all," said Woody.

"That's all he said. I'm hoping it isn't a waste of time."

"You and me both," Woody replied as he turned on the meter. He looked in the rearview mirror at the man in the back seat. "You should buckle up. The cops will give me a ticket if you don't."

"Sure, not a problem." Terry grabbed the seatbelt and buckled in.

"So. You some kind of reporter?"

"Excuse me?"

"I asked are you some kind of reporter?"

"Yeah, why do you ask?"

"You said something about a story at this shopping center. I know it's been closed for a couple of years now. There's no reason to go there; but you said there was a story there. Are they going to reopen the place?"

"I honestly don't know," Terry answered. "I was just told to go there and I would find a story."

"So you are a reporter."

"Yes, I work for the *City Times*."

Woody picked up a newspaper lying next to him. "Read it all the time."

"Thanks, appreciate the patronage."

They pulled into the empty parking lot of the shopping center. Woody drove through the parking lot. "Nothing here."

Terry pointed to side of the building. "It's around back. At least, that's what he said."

"Who said?"

"Some guy on the phone."

Woody stopped the taxi. "Listen guy, you had better not by leading me on a wild goose chase or trying to set me up. I know you're a midget, but how do I know you aren't leading me someplace where I'm going to get robbed?"

Terry took out his identification for the newspaper and handed the driver forty dollars. "I'm not going to rob you. I work at a newspaper. This morning we got a phone call saying something happened out here, and I came here to investigate. That's all."

"Why didn't you drive your own car?'

"I don't have one. I don't even have a driver's license."

"You don't know how to drive."

"I didn't say that. Look, I live in the city and I find it easier and cheaper to use public transportation than to own a car. Please, just drive to the rear and let's see if there is anything back there."

"Okay," Woody replied as he drove around to the back. They slowly moved along rear entrances of the deserted stores until they came to a pile of debris.

"You think this is it?" asked Woody.

"Don't know," Terry said as he slid out of the taxi. He hesitatingly walked to the pile. He quickly turned and ran back to Woody.

"Call the police," Terry shouted.

"Why? What's wrong?"

Terry point to the debris. "There's a dead girl over there. This is more than a story. It's murder."

~ ~ ~

From his vantage point, he could see the taxi pull around the shopping center and stop several feet from the debris pile. *They weren't the police, so who were they?* He watched as a short individual got out of the vehicle, walked over to the debris, and ran back to the driver. But they didn't leave. The short guy walked back over to debris pile and started taking pictures with his cell phone. *What a ghoul.* Within minutes, there were police vehicles with their blue lights flashing. Patrol officers began stretching yellow tape around the debris, using their vehicles as posts for the crime scene tape. He became delighted at the sight of news vans with TV cameras arrived, along with additional police cars. He was disappointed when the police put up a plastic tarp to prevent the press from getting pictures of the body. He went back to his blue pickup and reached into a cooler, pulling out a cold beer. This is better than the movies he thought as he took a long swig from the can he was holding.

~ ~ ~

Terry tried to think of a logical explanation why four police cruisers had their lights flashing while they secured the crime scene behind an abandon building. Who were they trying to warn? It did make it easy for TV news crews and newspaper reporters to find them. Unfortunately for

Terry, the *City Times* has sent Ashford to cover the story. Reporters were trying to find a position where they could get photos of the investigation. The police erected walls of blue plastic hiding the body and the crime scene from the eyes of the media.

Woody groaned as he sat back in the driver's seat. "We could be here for hours before they move the body and take our statements. And I'm hungry. Hey, just so you know, I'm still running the meter. You're going to owe me for waiting around here."

"Are you kidding," Terry exclaimed holding his hand out towards the blue tarp. "There's a dead woman over there and you're worried about getting paid."

"Damn right."

"I don't blame you," said a voice behind them.

Terry and Woody turned to face a man in chino slacks and a blue blazer. He had a detective's shield on his belt."

"I'm Detective Marshall. Nick Marshall. Need to talk to you about the body you found."

"He found it," Woody said pointing at Terry. "I'm just a taxi driver."

Marshall turned his attention to Terry. "So, tell me what brought you out here?"

Terry pulled his hands out of his pockets. "Earlier today I got a phone call. The person at the other end told me there was a story out here behind an abandon shopping center. I got a taxi to drive me out here, where I found the poor girl murdered, and I immediately called you."

"How do you know she was murdered?"

"With all of the blood on her clothes and the fact she was laying on a pile of debris, I *assumed* she was."

"Okay. What can you tell me about the person who called you?"

"Nothing," Terry replied. "I spoke to him for only a few seconds. He told me to look here and I would find a story. I looked, and I found the girl. That's it."

"That's it?"

"I think he used a machine to distort his voice. It didn't sound normal."

"Okay. So, why do you think he called you?"

"He didn't call me," Terry explained. "He called the paper. I just happened to answer the phone."

"Do you have any idea who might have called you?"

"No."

"Did you know the victim?"

"No."

"So as a journalist, you get a phone call and decide to check it out, on your own without reporting it to anyone?"

"Report what?" Terry said with a hint of frustration. "I can't call the police every time I get a strange phone call. You know how many nuts are out there?"

The detective chuckled. "Yeah, I do. I'm a cop. I deal with them on a daily basis."

"So do I," Terry replied.

"Hey man," interrupted Woody, "really, all we did was drive up and spot a dead girl. Then we called you. That's it. Is it okay if we go now?"

"Sure," answered Detective Marshall. "Just let me get your contact information and then you can go.

Chapter Two

She woke up sweating – again. Paula Stanford threw the sheets off her six-foot, two-inch frame and planted her feet on the floor. She wiped the sweat from her face down her shoulder-length blond hair. She got up looking around for the bottle of Jim Beam she had been drinking. She found it on the end table next to the chair facing the television.

Beneath the bottle was a small piece of paper with the word *muffin* on it. This was her clue. The doctors at the VA gave her pills to help with her insomnia. They worked very well. So well that she would sleep walk. One time she woke up the next morning to discover several hamburgers from a local fast-food place. The receipt showed she had purchased the hamburgers at two o'clock in the morning, but she had no memory of it. Since then, she started hiding her keys. She placed the keys in a lock box, then hid the lock box and the key, each night in a different place. Then, she would place a clue as to the location of the key to the lock box. Today's clue was *muffin,* which meant she hid the key to the lock box in the muffin tins she had in a kitchen drawer. For added security, she placed a stack of empty cans with small rocks in them in front of the door, hoping the noise from knocking them over would wake her. This way she kept from leaving the apartment. At least it gave her relief every morning to discover the cans had not been disturbed.

Her dilemma now was to take the pills and risk sleep walking or try to sleep without having nightmares. She closed her eyes. She was so tired, yet she could not sleep. Alcohol helped, but its relief was short-lived. She twisted the top off of the Jim Beam bottle but stopped short of taking a drink. A quick glance at the clock told her that her alarm would ring in less than two hours. No sense in going back to bed. Paula put the cap back on the bottle and got out her sweat pants. If she couldn't sleep, she might as well run.

~ ~ ~

The next morning as Terry sat at his desk going through photos of the dead girl on his cell phone. The photos showed a young woman, with multiple stab wounds to her abdomen and chest. Blood covered her dress. Her eyes stared vacantly into the air. It angered Terry the killer had dumped her in a pile of garbage. Terry had been very careful not to disturb anything at the scene. He put down his phone and picked up a picture of a pretty brunette from his desk.

"I miss you Kristen," Terry said to the photo. "I went out on a story yesterday and I found a dead girl. Strange, it was always news before, but now, it's different somehow. I mean I was a true reporter. I even got some photographs on my cell phone before the police arrived. But, it's not a story, it's not news. It's a poor girl whose parents are going to find out their daughter was murdered, and we add to the pain by making it a headline. We use it to get more readers, 'The more it bleeds, the more it reads.' When did the news become more about sensationalism than caring for the victims? How I wish you were here. You always knew how to cover the news and care about the people at the same time."

"Hey Runt. What are you doing?" Ashford said, walking up and banging the back of Terry's chair. "Talking to yourself?"

Terry put the photo of his wife back on his desk. "I was thinking about the dead girl I found yesterday."

"Looks like you were talking to your wife's picture. I can't believe such honey would marry someone like you. What was wrong with her?"

"Nothing was wrong with her," Terry shouted. "She was perfect. And you have no right to insult her.

"Listen runt. I don't care about her. What I want to know is who told you to go out and cover a story?"

"I did," Terry answered. "And if you remember, I told you about it before I went out."

"Yeah, yeah. Listen Runt, you're a copy editor. Your job is here, at this desk, not out there on the road. Stay in your lane."

"You mean stay here and let you get all of the glory for covering the news."

"Hey, I'm a reporter," Ashford said putting his hands to his chest before pointing to Terry. "You're an editor. That's your job."

"Gee, and here I thought it was *our* job to cover the news."

"You know what's worse than being short. It's being a smart ass."

"It's better than being a dumb ass."

"Knock it off you two," yelled a large man, also known as Bill Fitch the managing editor. "Both of you, make like the Jolly Green Giant and can the crap."

Ashford turned to Fitch and pointed to Terry. "Do you know what this runt did yesterday? He made a taxi driver take him around town…"

"And found a news story about a homicide," Terry answered before Ashford could finish his sentence. "Look, there's a real news story here."

Fitch started in the newspaper business when they still used teletypes, long before the age of personal computers. Like all editors, he started as a reporter, even spending time as a war correspondent, before earning a position on the editorial staff. He knew and had experienced personal conflicts in newsrooms. Fitch groaned and crossed his arms before responding to this one. "I know there is a story here, but Ashford's right. Your position is here at the copy desk. That's why I sent Ashford out there to handle the story. Besides, no one is as good as you for editing. I mean you're a wiz at grammar and rewriting. As for you Ashford, quit giving Terry trouble just because he found a story and you didn't. Now, both of you, get back to work." Fitch stood there, watching both of them.

Terry reluctantly returned to his desk and began to gently touch the photo on his desk.

"You still miss her, don't you?" Diana asked as she sat down next to Terry and passed him coffee in a Styrofoam cup. "How long has Kristen been gone?"

"Four years, three months, twelve days."

"It's been a long time. Maybe time for you to move on."

"I know, but it's hard. Kristen was the only one who saw me as a whole person, not some gag or trophy date. In high school, I was a joke. Girls would go out with me only to laugh about our *date* afterwards. I thought college would be different, but it wasn't, until I met Kristen. She made me feel like John Wayne."

Diana rubbed Terry's shoulder. "Well cowboy, it's time for you to get back in the saddle again."

"Are you asking me out on a date?" Terry said with some surprise.

"Well, I don't know Pilgrim," Diana said in her best John Wayne voice. Both Terry and Diana smiled at the silly imitation. "Look, I know you loved Kristen; but you should move on. Hey, some of my girlfriends and I are going to that Wild West Show at the fairgrounds this evening, why don't you join us."

"I don't know."

"It's friends getting together for some fun. Besides, I'm going to be there with three of my girlfriends, so joining us will not be any big deal."

"I know, but it's a girls' night out. I don't want to get in the way. I'll just be extra baggage." Terry replied.

"You're not *extra baggage*. And it's not really a girls' night out. It's coworkers getting together. Come on. Do something tonight other than going home to watch TV alone."

"Nah, I'd hate to butt in."

"What butting in. I'm asking you. All you're doing is meeting us at the fairgrounds. The worst that could happen is you join us for a drink afterwards. If the girl talk gets too much, you can always cut out on your own."

"Okay. I'll meet you there. When does the show begin?"

"It begins at eight, so try to hook up with us at around seven thirty."

~ ~ ~

Paula Stanford was in a bad mood. She usually was after her appointments with the mental health counselor at the VA. "Deep breaths," or "you should try meditation," wasn't what Paula wanted to hear when talking about her anger issues, depression, and insomnia. The VA had put her on drugs for her depression and anger problems, which proved ineffective. It took Paula months to finally lose the weight the medication made her gain. To make matters worse, she was late for her exercise class, and she hated to be late, mainly because she was the instructor. She hurried along the sidewalk, silently cursing while darting between slow moving pedestrians, trying not to hit anyone with her gym bag. She quickly looked down and made sure it was secure against her side. She didn't see the short man until she ran into him, knocking him down.

Terry, surprised at being bowled over, looked up at the tall blond woman standing over him.

"Sorry," the Amazon said with some frustration as she bent down to help Terry up.

"It's all right, I should have watched where I was going."

"No, I should have watched where I was going. Hope I

13

didn't hurt you." The woman still sounded hostile.

Terry blushed. "No, I'm fine."

Paula stood there for a moment, angry at herself for crashing into someone, trying to think of something to say.

"Really, I'm fine," Terry said to relieve the embarrassment of the situation.

"Again, I'm sorry. I'm in a bit of a rush and I didn't mean to knock you down. Are you sure you're all right? I didn't hurt you. Did I?" This time she sounded sincere.

Terry smiled and appreciated the change of tone in her voice. "Honestly, I'm fine. No problems."

The blond Amazon smiled. Terry could tell she was a bit embarrassed

"Yeah, well, take care. Again, sorry for knocking you down," she said.

"It's okay."

"Thank you for understanding." Paula nodded and continued on her way.

~ ~ ~

Bright lights, noise from carnival rides, and food wagons surprised Terry. He had expected to see cowboys riding horses and bulls in a dirt ring, not this transitory festival to the old West. Terry wandered through the crowd looking for Diana and her friends, a feat made considerable more difficult due to his height. Terry realized he was getting hungry and stepped up to a food truck serving corn dogs.

"Out of the way, shrimp," said a man dressed in blue jeans, a polo shirt, and a faded baseball cap, butting his way in front of Terry.

"Excuse me. But I was here first," Terry interjected

The individual wasn't particularly imposing. He was average height, which was almost two feet taller than Terry. He had a slight paunch and was unshaven. He barely gave Terry a glance before ignoring him and ordering two corn dogs. Terry realized the futility of pursuing the matter any further.

The man took his food and faced Terry. "Kiss off shrimp."

Terry and the vendor watched the man walk away. "Sorry about that," the vendor said. "I hate it when customers are rude to others. Hey, what can I do for you?"

Terry smiled and waved his hand. "It's okay. It's not your fault. Can I get two corn dogs and a Coke?"

"Sure thing." The vendor disappeared from the window, only to return a moment later with Terry's order. "Here you go. And here, have a pretzel on the house. You deserve it after the way that guy treated you."

"Thanks," Terry replied, accepting the vendor's hospitality. Terry finished his food and was sipping his drink when he spotted the offensive man from the vendor's stand talking to a young woman in a flowered summer dress and her friend. While he couldn't hear what was said, Terry could tell the women wanted the conversation to end, but the man did not. *Some people can't take a hint* Terry thought, and it was obvious that this individual was going to need bright lights, a large sign, and being hit with a taser before he realized the women didn't welcome his company.

Terry walked over to the group. "Do you ladies need some help?"

"Buzz off," the individual responded vehemently. "This is none of your business."

Terry shook his head slightly. "Well maybe I want to make it my business," Terry replied as he balled his fists. Terry quickly realized the foolishness of this act. He knew he could not defeat the rude man in any kind of physical confrontation. Still, he didn't back down."

The rude individual laughed at the challenge. "You walk away and we'll forget you were ever here."

"Hey," said the woman in a flowered dress. "Why don't we walk away? Really, no one wants any trouble, so let's all forget all of this."

The man turned as the women walked away, leaving him standing alone. Terry could see he was upset, which pleased Terry very much.

"I should beat the crap out of you," the individual said.

"You can, but it won't bring back the ladies. All it will do is get you thrown in jail for assault."

The individual walked away without saying a word.

Terry waved his fingers at the man's back. Terry continued to wander through the festival atmosphere, looking for Diana. He stopped and tried his hand at a dart game hoping to win a prize he could conveniently give to Diana. He wasn't successful. Minutes later, he saw the rude individual again, this time talking to Diana and several of her friends.

Terry and walked up to the group. "Can I help you ladies?" Terry asked.

"Terry," Diana exclaimed happily. "Good to see you. We've been waiting for you."

"You've been waiting for him?" the unpleasant individual said pointing to Terry. "What do you want with a shrimp when you can have a real man?"

"You really do have a problem with people, don't you?" Terry said stepping in front of the individual.

Diana forced her way between Terry and the rude individual. "Well, he's our friends and we promised we would spend the evening with him. Sorry, but we really do need to keep our promise."

"Yeah, yeah. I get it. It's a pity date for the shrimp." To everyone's relief, the unpleasant man left.

"Don't listen to him," Diana said "I'm glad you came along. You provided a good excuse to get rid of him. Come on in. It should be a fun show."

~ ~ ~

Paula forced a smile as she waved her arms to the beat of the music which she could barely hear over the noise from carnival rides. She couldn't pass up this opportunity to promote the gym where she worked and hopefully recruit new members. What she really couldn't pass up the opportunity to earn extra money for doing the demonstration. The audience had been sparse during the performance of the main attraction in the arena. Now that it was over, more people had joined. Below the stage were several young boys watching her. Paula made it a point to smile and give them a small wave of her hand. The boys giggled and whispered to each other. Paula was sure it was some stupid juvenile joke, probably about her height. She wanted to jump off the stage, grab the kids by the throat, and demand to know what they were laughing at. Instead she kept smiling and dancing. The music ended and a few members in the audience clapped their hands. Paula picked up a towel and wiped the sweat from her face.

"Thank you all for attending," Paula addressed the meager audience. "Be sure to come by our gym on Broad Street for a free lesson and more information about our programs. We have information on our programs and rates here for your convenience." The audience slowly disappeared from the front of the stage. The smile slowly faded from Paula's face. She had gotten warmer receptions from the DMV. The carnival was shutting down for the evening, and the stage hands were anxious to finish their work and find a nearby bar where they could complain about cheap pay, cheap customers, and cheap politicians. She envied them. She didn't care about the cheap customers or the cheap politicians, but she certainly could use a drink. Paula thanked those who performed with her. Within a few minutes, she stood alone; even the stage hands had finished and were gone. She grabbed her gym bag, the remaining pamphlets, and started towards her car.

~ ~ ~

The unpleasant man made his way to his car. He was still

upset at that dwarf interrupting him when he was talking to the young women at the arena. That dwarf was the same one who had interrupted him earlier when he was talking to those other two women. Not that it mattered, he found that lady in the flowered dress alone. She had become separated from her friend. She still didn't want to talk to him. Well, he fixed that. He taught her a lesson. He actually enjoyed what he did to her. He wished he could have done something to teach the shrimp a lesson too. Maybe he would get the opportunity later. He took out his keys. He didn't have time to look for the dwarf, he had to leave.

He backed up his pickup truck. Suddenly, he felt a jolt and heard a crash. *Damn it* he thought as he looked in rear view mirror. He had run into a parked car behind him. *Better leave before someone see me,* the individual thought as he put the truck into drive. Tires spun wildly, kicking up dirt as he sped away.

~ ~ ~

Paula had to jump back to avoid being hit by a blue pickup truck. "Hey, look where you're going," she yelled the single taillight moving away from her. She cursed at the truck as it skidded around some cars and accelerated. It skidded around another row of cars. The driver kept going and was soon out of sight.

Paula continued on her way. She groaned when she got to her car. Someone had run into it, smashing the right front fender and headlight. She just knew in her bones it was the truck that almost hit her. It was like twisted Karma. Fortunately, she could still drive the car. Unfortunately, it was going to cost her more than she could afford to get it repaired.

18

Chapter Three

Terry appreciated the busy pace of the newsroom. He finished editing one story and the next one appeared. It made the day go faster. The deadline was six hours away, but he had everything under control. Then the phone rang interrupting his concentration.

"*City Times*, copy editing, can I help you."

"I'm helping you," crackled the distorted voice at the other end.

Terry stiffened. He recognized the voice from the other day. "Yeah, well that's great. What are you going to do to help me?"

"I've got another news story for you. Did you like my last one?"

"It made the front page," Terry said secretly hoping it wouldn't encourage him to commit another murder, at the same time hoping the killer would give himself away.

"What about the one last night? Will it make the front page?"

"What are you talking about?"

"The one last night at the fairgrounds."

Terry took a deep breath. "You're going to tell me that you kill someone else. Too late. It's old news. The police are on top of it. Besides, I think they have someone in custody."

"You're lying," the voice said vehemently. "No one saw me. So quit playing games with me if you want the story. Or don't you?"

"Yes, yes, of course. Please. Tell me about last night."

"The police haven't found last night's victim. If they had,

it would be on the news. That means she's still out there."

"Where can I find her?"

"I don't think I'll tell you. You'll have to go find her yourself. Ride them cowboy." The voice hung up.

Terry replaced the receiver of the phone and reached for his wallet. He pulled out the detective's card and dial the number on it. Someone at the other end answered. "This is Terry Lambert. I need to talk to Detective Marshall."

~ ~ ~

Detective Nick Marshall had a routine. He started each day by reading his email and drinking coffee. He hated it when his routine was interrupted, so he was in a very unpleasant mood when someone told him he had a phone call. His mood was about to get worse. He picked up his phone. "Detective Marshall," was all he said.

"This is Terry Lambert. We met the other day when I found the body of a young lady behind the shopping center."

"Yeah, I remember you."

"I just got a call from the same person. He said there was another body at the fairgrounds."

~ ~ ~

He was disappointed. The fairgrounds were too open, so his vantage point was quite far away. He wouldn't be able to hide among the workers. They all knew each other. Also, if anyone had caught him at the fairgrounds, he would become an immediate suspect; something he couldn't allow. Fortunately, he had the foresight to bring a pair of binoculars to watch the police as they arrived. He noticed a very short person getting out of one of the vehicles. He wondered if it was the same one he had seen at the first crime scene. That person seemed very familiar, like they had met before. He smiled. He knew why the short guy looked so familiar. The police divided up into three groups. He watched them fan out. He realized he wouldn't see them find the body. He was disappointed. He would miss the excitement, but he knew what would happen, so he returned to his truck and left.

~ ~ ~

"All right," Detective Marshall said as he let Terry out of the back of the police vehicle. "We're here at the fairgrounds. You said there was a second victim." Several other police officers gathered around Marshall and Terry.

"No, I said someone called me on the phone and said there was a second victim," Terry answered. "I believe him. It was the same person who told me about the first victim behind the shopping center. He had the same strange voice, like it was being distorted by a machine. I think we need to search the area to find her."

"Okay, Okay," the detective acknowledged with the enthusiasm of someone getting a root canal from a dentist who had ran out of Novocain. "Harrison, you take two officers and start at the north entrance. Campbell, take two and start at the south entrance. Work in a counterclockwise direction. In the meantime, I'll take our witnesses and two patrolmen and start at the arena."

For two hours, everyone searched, but no one found a body. Frustrated, Terry sat down on the bleachers in the arena.

"Well no body," said the detective as he approached Terry.

"He had to hide the body somewhere," Terry said. "He hid it, but it wasn't found. Still he wants it found. That's why he called me. He wants us to find the body."

"But he didn't tell you where."

"The only thing he told me was there was a second victim."

"Anything else?"

"He said 'ride them cowboy'.'"

"We've searched the stables. There's nothing there but the horses."

"What about the bulls? Did you search their pens?" Terry asked.

Detective Marshall sighed and put his hands on his hips. "Give me a break. Of course, we searched them."

Terry blushed. He took a handkerchief from his jacket pocket and wiped the sweat from his brow. "She has to be here somewhere. What else do cowboys ride?"

One female patrol officer answered, "All the cowboys I knew rode Jeeps and pickup trucks."

"Horses, bulls, buckboards, covered wagons," another one of the patrol officers answered.

Terry raised his head, "and stagecoaches."

Terry, the detectives, and patrol officers rushed over to the stagecoach outside the arena. One patrol officer opened the door and looked in. "Nothing here."

Another officer climbed up to the top of the coach. "Same here, nothing."

Terry glanced under the wagon, seeing nothing, moved to the back. He saw a large stain on the canvas cover. "What about here? In this cargo space?

Detective Marshall unfastened the leather straps holding the canvas cover in place. He lifted the canvas flap and the body of a young woman fell onto the ground.

"You were right," Marshall said. "There was a second victim.

~ ~ ~

This time the flashing lights were limited to the coroner's vehicle. Patrol officers stretched plastic yellow tape around several poles creating a huge circle with the stagecoach in the center. Outside of the tape were officers, interviewing the members of the show.

Terry watched two members of the coroner's office carefully place the body in a black plastic bag, load it onto a gurney, and wheel it over to the vehicle waiting to take the victim away. Several crime scene technicians were examining the stagecoach in hopes of finding clues.

"I recognize her from last night, because of the flower dress." Terry said as the coroner's vehicle left the fairgrounds.

"So, tell me about last night," Marshall demanded as he pulled out a small notebook and pen.

"There isn't much to tell. I saw a guy harassing her and her friend," said Terry.

"Why don't you tell me about this person? The guy hassling women."

"Certainly," Terry answered. "I only saw him briefly. He was a male Caucasian, about thirty-years-old, medium height and weight. He had a beard, but it wasn't very full, kind of scruffy. He was wearing a dark polo shirt and jeans."

"Do you think you would recognize him if you saw him again.

"I'm sure I could."

"Was there anything distinctive about him?"

"Well, I remember he was very rude. He cut in front of me at a food truck earlier that evening."

"So, you remember him because he made you wait for your food?"

"No, it was more than that."

"What do you mean?"

"He called me 'shrimp'."

"All right, I can see why you wouldn't recommend him for Mr. Congenitally."

"Yeah, he was really rude," Terry emphasizing the statement. "He kept trying to hit on the ladies, even though they didn't want anything to do with him."

Marshall sighed. "That's it. It isn't much. I mean he's a person of interest; but being rude and obnoxious doesn't mean he's the killer. Still, it wouldn't hurt to check him out. I can hook you up with a police artist and maybe we can get a sketch of the individual. Do you want to do that?"

"Absolutely."

~ ~ ~

After two hours at the police station, Terry realized he couldn't tell what kind of eyes, or nose, or mouth the individual had. He could see the person's face clearly, but every time the artist put the features together, it was a different person. The artist and Terry agreed, this was not working.

Terry left the interview room and took a seat in one of the chairs along the wall of the detectives' rooms.

"Hey stranger."

Terry looked up to find the tall Amazon who had bowled him over the day before. "Oh hi. How are you doing?"

"Okay. I've had better days."

"I know what you mean," Terry said. "By the way, I'm Terry Lambert. We didn't get a chance to introduce ourselves last time."

"Sorry about that," the tall blond said as she sat down next to Terry. "I'm Paula, Paula Stanford. So why are you here?"

"There was a homicide last night at the fairgrounds."

"And you're a suspect," Paula said snickering.

"No, nothing like that. I remembered a guy who hassled the victim last night. I think maybe he did it."

"Why?"

"Well, I ran into him earlier in the evening. He cut in front of me when I was getting some food and he called me a shrimp. And again, when I ran into him later, he was a bit of an ass."

"So, the guy was a jerk; that doesn't mean he's a killer. I mean you have to be really warped to kill someone who doesn't want to talk to you."

"You're right, but this guy is warped."

"Who? The killer or the guy hassling you?"

"The killer."

"How do you know?"

"He's called me, twice."

"Wait a minute. You know who killed these women?"

"No, it's not like that. I work at a newspaper. The person who killed these women called me. He wanted to make sure the newspaper printed the story about the murders."

"And you think the person who called you is the same one you saw last night."

"I don't know. Maybe yes, maybe no. All I know is that guy last night was nasty and a jerk and the person who called the paper is one too."

"Sorry to disappoint you; but being a jerk doesn't make you a criminal. Trust me I know. I dealt with a lot of them."

Terry sighed and realized Paula was probably right. "What brings you here?"

"A traffic accident. Some *jerk* hit my car in the parking lot last night. I needed to file a report for insurance. The officer downstairs sent me up here to talk to one of the detectives. I have to give them my statement, which is probably totally useless. Still, it's my guess, they are looking into everything that happened last night in the hopes of getting a lead on *your* homicide."

Terry sat up. "So, they think the person who hit your car is the killer."

Paula smiled at him. "Look, the odds of the two events being connected are extremely remote. I'm talking like winning the lottery remote. But in the off chance they are, the police will look into everything. Unfortunately, the only thing I can tell them was a blue pickup truck almost ran me down, and I think it may have been the same vehicle that hit my car. I don't even know what kind it was. It could have been a Ford, a Chevy, a Dodge Ram for all I know. All I know is someone hit my car and now I have a smashed fender that's going to cost me a bundle to get fixed."

"Sorry to hear that."

"Yeah, well that's life. I hope they can get to me soon. I have a class in an hour."

"Oh, what are you taking?"

The tall blond put her hand on Terry's shoulder. "I'm not taking it, I'm teaching it. I'm a fitness instructor. I work down the street from where I first *bumped* into you." Paula picked up her gym bag.

"How did you get into that," Terry asked in hope of extending the conversation.

"I like to exercise, and I have basically no job skills. So, guess what, I found probably the only job I'm qualified for."

"I sincerely doubt that."

A detective came out and signaled for Paula to follow him.

"Finally. Hey, take care."

Terry waved to her as she walked away. He realized he needed to return to work.

~ ~ ~

"Where have you been?" Bill Fitch, the managing editor, demanded. "We've got copy that needs to get laid out for tomorrow's paper."

"I've been chasing down a story," Terry answered. "It turns out last night there was a homicide at the fairgrounds."

"Yeah, we know," Fitch replied. "Ashford's got the story already. It on your desk."

"But it's incomplete," Terry added."

Ashford rushed over from his desk. "What are you talking about Runt?"

"Stop calling me runt."

"Yeah, yeah. Ashford stop calling Terry a runt," Fitch said impatiently. "Now explain how you know about the second homicide."

"You remember the first one behind the shopping center. The one where I got a phone call telling me about it."

26

"Yeah," answered Fitch.

"Well, I got a second call this morning, from the same guy. He told me there was a second one at the fairgrounds. So, I told the police about the phone call. I got to go with them when they searched the fairgrounds. I was there when they found the body. These two homicides are connected; they have the same killer."

"Great," Fitch shouted. "Get over there and write it up for tomorrow's edition. We'll beat everyone to the punch; the only ones with the complete story. Good work Terry. I'll get Carl to finish up copyediting."

Terry gave Fitch a nod and hurried over to his desk. *I'm writing again Kristen* Terry said to himself as he ran his fingers over the photograph on his desk.

Ashford waited until Fitch was in his office before going over to Terry, who was at his desk. "What are you doing?" Ashford asked with a hiss leaning over Terry. "That was my story."

"What do you mean?" asked Terry as he set down the photo in his hand. "There was no story until I helped the police find the body."

"Are you trying to embarrass me, show me up, impress the brass with your ability? Well it won't work. You got lucky this time but watch it. You're playing with fire and you could get burnt."

"You're jealous because twice in one week you dropped the ball. As for showing you up, a girl scout with crayons could do that."

Ashford straightened up. "Watch yourself Runt. You may be taking on more than you can handle." Before Terry could reply, Ashford left.

~ ~ ~

Paula grabbed the half-empty bottle. She leaned back on the couch, reached for the glass on the table beside her, and pour herself a full two ounces of whiskey. She took a look at the amber liquid in the glass and poured another two ounces.

"Had a really bad day," she said to a photo of six Marines wearing desert camouflage uniforms and leaning against a Humvee. "Last night some jerk ran into my car and smashed my fender. Then I had to spend the day at the police station filing a report because someone was murdered last night at the fairgrounds where I was putting on a demonstration. Here I thought, I found the perfect job, teaching aerobics to housewives and office workers looking to lose weight. No bloodshed. No firefights. No violence. *Then* there's a dead body. You know what's the worst thing about it? I don't care about the dead person. I care about the jerk who ran into my car. I want his ass. But the killer, that's someone else's problem. What's wrong with me?"

Paula took a gulp and shallowed half the liquid in the glass. She sighed, picked up the whiskey bottle, and drained the glass before pouring more whiskey into it.

~ ~ ~

Although it was not his usual habit, Terry joined several reporters at Murphy's, a bar popular with journalists throughout the city, mainly because of free popcorn and two for the price of one happy hour.

Diana weaved her way through the crowd to the bar and ordered a couple of cocktails. Terry with a mug of beer in each hand came up to her. "I was going to offer you a beer, but I see you already have your drinks."

Diana turned to Terry, "heard you broke a major story today."

Terry blushed and took a sip of beer. "Not really. I got lucky. Remember the other day I told you about that strange phone call?"

"The one you went out on and found that dead girl?"

"Yeah, that's the one. Well, he called again today."

"What did you do?" Diana asked.

"I contacted the police of course. I went out and helped them find the second victim. Since I was there, I got the scoop before anyone else. I wrote it up and broke the story. Isn't it great? Maybe I'll get an award or something."

"Wait a minute," Diana interrupted. "Terry, are you telling me the killer calls you when he commits a murder? Do you know what that means?"

"Yeah, we'll always get the story first."

Diana sighed and put her hand on Terry's shoulder. "No, it means is the killer has singled you out as his point of contact. He is taunting the police, and you are in great danger."

"Why? He doesn't know who I am. He calls the copy desk and by chance I've answered the phone both times. All he knows is that someone at the paper answers the phone."

"Right now, that's all he knows," Diana said. "But soon he is going to find out it's you who answered the phone; and after that, the killer is going to demand to speak to you. And that places you in a very dangerous position."

"Well, what are we supposed to do?" Terry asked. "We have to help the police. It is the only way to stop him."

"Be very careful. I don't want you to get hurt. I would hate for you to make the headlines as one of his victims. I want you to be careful, and I mean very, very careful."

Terry took a big gulp of his beer and smiled at Diana. Neither of them noticed Ashford standing less than three feet away.

Chapter Four

"Excuse me," Terry said to the police officer behind the bulletproof glass pane. "I was here yesterday talking to Detective Marshall about the murder that took place at the fairgrounds."

"So, you need to talk to him again?"

"If it would be possible, yes."

The officer picked up the phone and called someone. Terry couldn't hear what was said, but the officer nodded agreement and hung up the receiver. "Detective Marshall said he'll be right with you." The officer pointed to a bench for Terry to wait.

Marshall appeared from behind a door. "Heard you were down here. What can I do for you?"

"I was wondering how it's going? The case that is."

Marshall motioned for Terry to follow him. He took Terry into one of five interview rooms. "Take a seat," Marshall said. "What do you want to tell me?"

"Nothing. I mean it's your case. I just want to know if you had any leads or anything."

"If I did, I wouldn't tell the press."

"No, no. I'm not here as a reporter. I'm here as a concerned citizen; someone who wants to help you catch the killer."

Marshall took a moment before replying. "I appreciate that, but police work needs to be left to the police. We're trained to handle it. When civilians get involved, they often end up as victims, complicating matters, and making more work for us."

Terry held up his hands in front of him. "I'm sorry, but I think there is some miscommunication here. I don't want to become involved in the investigation. It's just that this crazy guy has called twice and both times someone was murdered. I want to do everything I can to help you. Right now, I'm just curious how the investigation is going."

"Well, we have your statements, as well as the woman's..."

"Who?"

Marshall smiled. "The night of the second murder, a woman had her car smashed in by a hit and run. She gave us a vague description of a vehicle of a person of interest. Until we locate this person, there isn't much more I can say."

"Was this a tall, blond woman?

"I'm not at liberty to say. Look, I appreciate everything you've done and of course if you come across anything else, I want you to contact us. But for right now, please, leave police work to us. Okay?"

Terry nodded his head in agreement, knowing that his role in the case was far from over.

~ ~ ~

"Good morning. Can I help you," asked a pretty young lady behind a counter. "Welcome to our gym."

Terry looked around the foyer. He could see the doors to several exercise rooms, as well as the entrances to the men's and women's locker rooms. "Is there a woman named Paula who works here?"

"Sure, you need to see her? She's between classes right now. Give me a minute and I'll get her for you." The young lady disappeared into one of the exercise rooms. She returned a few seconds later. "She'll be right out."

Before Terry could respond, Paula came out, wiping her hands with a small towel. "Hey," she said acknowledging Terry with a nod of her head. "What can I do for you?"

"When I met you yesterday at the police station, you said you had been in an accident."

"No, I said some jerk ran into my car. While I was giving demonstrations at the fairgrounds, someone hit my car and took off. I found a smashed fender and a busted headlight when I got back to my car."

"Any idea of who did it?"

"Nope."

"But I thought you said someone in a pickup truck did it."

"No, I said a jerk in a blue pick up almost ran me down, and I wouldn't be surprised if it was the same one who ran into my car. I didn't see anyone hit my car, but there were some bits of blue paint on the fender."

"So the killer drives a blue pickup. That's a clue."

Paula let out a heavy sigh. "You have been watching too much *CSI*. Someone smashed my fender. Someone driving a blue pickup almost ran me down. Someone killed a young woman. There is no reason to think these events are connected. If by some strange chance they are, the police will find out and they will handle it."

"Don't you want to find the killer?"

"No, I want to find the person who smashed my fender."

"But they're the same person."

"Why, because they both happened at the fairgrounds. I'll bet there were fights, pickpockets, other fender benders. Just because they happen at the same place doesn't mean they are connected."

Paula could see Terry was disappointed.

Terry looked around, trying to avoid direct eye contact. Then he faced Paula. "So, you won't help me."

"Help you how?

"I don't know," Terry answered.

"Same here," Paula replied. "Look, it's great that you want to help catch the killer and put him behind bars. But there really isn't anything we can do except let the police do their job."

~ ~ ~

Terry kept staring at his computer screen, still disappointed from his earlier conversation with Paula.

"Hey Runt."

"Stop that," Terry demanded as he turned around to face Ashford. "What do you want?"

Ashford leaned over Terry and picked up the picture of Kristen. "I still can't believe a hot babe like this married you."

Terry grabbed the photograph from Ashford's hands. "Leave that alone. It's private. Now, what do you want?"

"Any calls this morning? Has your favorite news source called you?"

"No, thank goodness."

"What?" Ashford said with mock surprise. "You don't want him to call you?"

"Of course not. Every time he calls, it's to tell me he's killed someone. I want him caught and put away, not running around killing people, although I could make an exception if it were you."

"Watch yourself Runt."

"Or what? You'll say something irritating. Too late, it's already happened."

"So when do you think your favorite fan will call?"

"Hopefully never. If we're lucky, he'll get run over by a bus."

"Can I quote you on that?"

"No, I don't want to be part of the story."

"Too late. It's your byline on the story about the second murder. It isn't going to take the killer long to realize you're the person he talked to on the phone." Ashford was smiling when he left Terry to continue his work.

"Don't listen to him," Diana said as she sat down next to

Terry. "Need you to review the story I sent in yesterday,"

"Which one?"

"The one on veterans coming back from Iraq. I'm focusing on the issues they have readjusting to civilian life."

"Yeah, I guess it's really hard."

"You wouldn't believe some of the stories I've heard," Diana said as she pulled out several photos. "Some of these vets aren't just physically injured, they're emotionally maimed as well."

Terry grabbed one of the photos. "Hey, I know this person."

"Yeah, she's kind of special," Diana answered. "Her name is Paula Stanford. I tried to interview her, but she refused. Her response was 'it's better to leave everything that happened over there, over there, and not bring it home.' I heard from another Marine who served with her that she was a real war hero, saved several lives."

"How is she doing now?" Terry asked.

Diana took the photo from Terry's hand and placed it back with the others. "As far as I can tell, she's just existing until she feels she can find a way to rejoin the human race."

~ ~ ~

It had been another rough night for Paula. She tried to avoid taking the sleeping pills, but at two in the morning, she realized she needed to get some sleep, and it wasn't coming without the use of medication. Medication made it hard to get up and get going. Paula knew she would need a lot of coffee.

Paula didn't like the pretentious people she often found at Le Rue, a sidewalk café near the gym. They would drink their specially ordered coffee or tea, snack on over-priced pasties, talk about topics in hopes of impressing people sitting across from them. Then there were people like the jerk sitting at the table next to her. He had his headphones on, but his music was so loud, she could hear it. Didn't people realize listening to music that loudly would hurt your hearing. Not that she cared about his hearing. She was annoyed because this person's inconsideration forced her to listen to his music. Paula wanted to rip the headphones off his head and smack him eight or nine times. The words of her therapist kept coming back to her. *You can't control others; you can only control you.* Paula remembered the therapist's advice. *Breathe deeply, count, then exhale; and repeat the process until you calm down.* Paula took a deep breath, counted, and still heard the music. It wasn't working.

The annoying individual got up and left. Paula tried the breathing exercises again. She took in a deep breath, held it, and let it out. That's when she saw Terry walking down the sidewalk, lost in thought. Just like that unwelcomed music, the therapist's advice invaded Paula's mind. *You need to get out more and meet new people.* The therapist was becoming as annoying as people who played their music too loud and dating site advertisements on the internet. For some strange reason, this time Paula took her therapist's advice. "Hey stranger," she called out.

Terry looked around. He saw a tall blond waving at him. It took a moment before he realized she was the woman who knocked him down a couple of day ago, and the same one he met at the police station two days ago. Terry stood on the other side of the black, wrought iron barrier separating the sidewalk tables and pedestrian traffic. Paula realized she really didn't know what to say next. "Why don't you join me?" she asked surprising herself.

Terry took a quick look at his watch. "Why not? I've got the time." He disappeared into the café and returned a few minutes later holding a latte and chicken sandwich."

"Lunch or breakfast?" Paula inquired looking at her watch.

"A bit of both," Terry answered. "It's not much, but it's

enough for me. How about you?"

"Breakfast," she replied holding up a cup of coffee. "It was a rough night and I need this to get going. The good thing is my gym is about a block from here, so I can come back if I need more."

Terry unwrapped his sandwich. "So, what made you become a fitness teacher?"

"Long story."

"Do you mind if I ask what's it is?"

"Only if you tell me yours."

Terry took a bite of his sandwich. "Sure," he said with his mouth full. "But you first. I heard you used to be in the military."

"Not much to tell. I served six years as a military police officer for the Marine Corps. The first four years was at Quantico, where I was basically a patrol officer, then ended up as an investigator. I got sent over to Iraq. I was there for about four months when the convoy I was with got attacked. I got wounded and spent most of a year in hospitals and physical therapy. I finish my enlistment as a criminal investigator. When I got out, I really didn't have any job skills except for exercising, so I ended up an aerobics instructor. I like it. The exercise helps me deal with stress and anxiety."

"Why didn't you become a cop?"

"That's another story, for another time. What's your story?"

Terry swallowed a mouthful of his sandwich and took a sip of his latte. "I work as a copy editor for *City Times*. I've been there for twelve years, ever since I graduated college."

"That's it?" Paula said with a bit of disappointment. "Are you married? Do you have kids? Pets? How did you get into the newspaper business?" Come on, I want details."

Terry let out a small laugh. "All right, I get it, it's the third degree. Okay. I have always been interested in journalism, which I majored in when I was in college. So of course, after college, I tried being a reporter. But being a dwarf, few people took me seriously. However, the managing editor realized I was very good at writing, so he made me a copy editor. I like the job. The paper was nice enough to get me a special chair and make sure my work station fit my size. That's it."

"No, no, no," Paula said waving her finger at Terry. "Tell me about your personal life. Are you married? Do you have a family? Do have pets? Hobbies?"

Terry looked down at the ground. "I was married. But that's a story for another time."

"You still miss her, don't you?'

"Yeah, I do. How do you know?"

"It's the way you interact with others. It seems you want to be friendly, but you aren't looking for any kind of emotional relationship. And you still wear your wedding ring."

Terry put his sandwich down, wiped his hands on a napkin, and took a sip from his latte. "It's hard to explain, but it's hard to let go of someone you cared for."

"I've been through the same thing with people I served with. You become really close to those who you serve with in combat. They become family."

"What about you? Any family outside of the military?" Terry asked.

"Nope, not married. No boyfriend, and yes, I am heterosexual. But really, look at me. I'm six feet two inches tall and not exactly good looking, so finding a significant other has always proven to be difficult. As for a family, my parents along with my two sisters live in Ohio. Here, the closest thing I have to any relationship is a potted plant."

Terry took another bite of his sandwich before putting it down on the table between them. "You know, one of the things they teach us in journalism is often there is more to the story than what is said. I'm sure that's the case with you. You're not unattractive. As for being tall, I think you're a nice person; and

I know there are people out there who see you for who you really are and don't care about your height."

Paula took a sip of her coffee. "I come with too much emotional baggage for anyone looking for a relationship. If I told you I was nuts, I would be flattering myself. I'm nowhere close to being that sane."

"Don't let it bother you," said a voice on the other side of the barrier separating the sidewalk tables from pedestrians. "Most people who deal with him end up nuts."

Paula and Terry looked up to see Ashford standing there. "Introduce me to your friend," Ashford requested.

Terry pointed to Ashford. "Paula, met Ashford Zane, one of the reporters at the *City Times* and a real pain in the ass."

"Don't you believe it," Ashford said extending his hand to Paula. "I am a reporter, but not a pain in the ass."

"Paula, Paula Stanford."

"So how do you know Terry?"

"She was at the fairgrounds when the second woman was murdered," Terry answered. "It turns out the killer smashed into her car."

"Not quite," Paula countered. "I was at the fairgrounds the night of the murder, but I didn't see anything. That same night, someone ran into my car. But he left before I got there, so it was a hit and run. The odds of the two being connected are slim, real slim, pencil thin."

"So, you have nothing to do with the murder investigation."

"That's right," Paula answered taking a quick look at her watch. "Sorry to cut this short, but I have to get to work."

Terry extended his hand. "It was good to see you again."

Paula shook Terry's hand and waved to Ashford. "Good to see you too. Take care."

Chapter Five

Paula sat in her car. She wished the smashed front fender would somehow repair itself and she wouldn't have to walk into the auto repair shop office. The VA therapist kept telling her to envision things the way she hoped they would be. She closed her eyes and willed it to happen. After a minute, she opened her eyes to the disappointment of the fender still being bent out of shape. Once again that therapist had failed her. No, it wasn't the therapist's fault, and she knew it. She forced herself to open the car door and walk across the parking lot to the auto repair shop's office.

"How can I help you?" a man with the name "Ed" stitched over the left pocket of his blue, work shirt asked Paula as she stepped into the office.

"I need to get my fender repaired," Paula stated. "Someone ran into it a couple of nights ago in a parking lot."

"You got insurance?" Ed asked.

"Yeah, but I also have a thousand-dollar deductible, so I need an estimate on what's it going to cost."

"No problem. Let's look at it."

Paula led Ed out to her car. "I can drive it, so the damage is mostly cosmetic. But, I'm afraid if I don't get it repaired, the fender will fall off."

"Nah, it will stay on." Ed ran his hand over the fender before standing back up. "Tell you what. I think I can find you another fender and headlight to replace these from a junkyard I do some business with. All I'll have to do is take these off, put the others on, and paint it. That way it will probably cost you less than three hundred, certainly no more than that."

"Can you guarantee that price?"

Ed smiled at Paula. "If I can get that fender and headlight, sure thing. Whatever happens, I'll be sure to give you an accurate estimate before I start any work."

"I appreciate that."

"No problem. I understand your situation. I feel if I treat my customers right, they help me out by referring me to their friends."

"If you treat me right, I certainly will."

~ ~ ~

Terry thought about removing the phone from his desk. Each time it rang, Terry cringed at answering it. At the end of the day Terry didn't know whether to be relieved the voice hadn't called or to be disappointed, fearing he had moved onto another news source. Each morning, Terry came into work, hoping for and dreading a call from the voice. This morning, everyone's attention was focused on a particular news story.

Fitch demanded Terry come into his office as soon as Terry walked in. Fitch had Terry take a seat before handing him a copy a rival newspaper, which featured Terry and his role in the investigation of the homicides on the front page.

"How did this happen?" Terry demanded. "I'm not supposed to be in the news. And what is this about a lead from the night of the second murder?"

"I don't know," Fitch replied. "All I know is now everyone, including the killer, knows who you are; this places you in a very unusual position."

Terry handed the story back to Fitch. "What, am I in danger?"

Fitch sat down behind his desk. "Well let's not panic. The killer established a connection with you. He'll call us first. Hopefully, he will continue to call us and not the paper that printed the story."

"The guy is a serial killer," Terry shouted. "Who cares about the story? We need to help the police catch this guy."

"Look, I understand you're upset, and I don't blame you. Of course, we will work with the police to catch this guy. But look at this way. Right now, you are the link between him and the world. We have an obligation to inform the public about this guy and what he wants."

"What he wants is to kill people."

Fitch ran his hands over his face. "I'm not handling this very well. Let me try again. This guy is news. You are his connection with the world. We need to maintain that connection so that we can inform the public of the reasons for his actions. Maybe that way we can keep people safe."

"No," Terry answered standing up and pounding Fitch's desk with his fist. "What we need to do is everything we can to help the police find him and put him away."

"Of course," Fitch replied. "And we will do that. But I need you to keep talking to this guy."

"I still want to know how this other paper found out who I was and my connection to the killer."

"Terry, how do you think it happened? Someone told them, probably for a favor or money. It's too late now to worry about that. We need to focus on keeping in touch with him and following the story."

Terry looked out the glass window of Fitch's office. He had a very good idea who told the other paper about him. Terry turned back to face Fitch. "Here's what I'm going to do. If he calls again, first thing I will do is inform the police. I won't hold anything back from the cops."

"Wouldn't think of it."

"And I write the stories. No one else. This is my scoop."

"Terry, it's been years since you were on the street. Do you think that's wise? Things have changed since then."

"No, they haven't, and I don't care. I'm a trained reporter and a damn good writer. I write the stories."

"Okay, you got it. But if you need any help, let me know and I'll get someone to lend you a hand."

Terry stormed out of the office and over to his desk.

Ashford waited until Terry logged onto his computer. "Hey, saw you made the papers."

Terry glared at Ashford. "That shouldn't surprise you."

"What do you mean?"

"My grandfather told me a story about a farmer, a salesman, and a jackass."

"What's this got to do with this morning's news?"

Terry ignored the question. "It turns out this salesman was walking down a road when he came upon a farmer and a jackass in a field. The salesman said 'Good morning" to the farmer, and he said the same back. Then the jackass bayed at the salesman. The salesman turned to the farmer and asked what the jackass said. The farmer looked at the salesman and told him the jackass didn't say anything; it's a jackass. The salesman nodded to the farmer and started to turn away. The jackass bayed again. Again, the salesman asked the farmer what the jackass said. Again, the farmer told the salesman the jackass said nothing; it's a jackass. The salesman turned to walk away, and the jackass bayed again. The salesman demanded to know what the jackass said. The farmer said that this time the jackass did say something."

"Yeah, what did the jackass say?" Ashford inquired with a chuckle.

"The jackass said that only a fool would listen to a jackass. I'm no fool."

"Are you calling me a jackass?"

"Of course not. It would be an insult to the jackass."

Ashford began to blush as others in the newsroom began to giggle. "Watch it Runt. You've got a lot to lose if you're not careful."

Terry couldn't help himself. He was grinning ear to ear

when Ashford walked away. He noticed Diana gave him a thumbs-up gesture.

~ ~ ~

The routine at the paper was simple. Reporters wrote their stories and had another reporter review them for any errors they may have overlooked. Afterwards, the reporters corrected the errors and turned their stories over to Terry, who reviewed and edited them. Hardly exciting. The excitement came when Detective Marshall with two others came into the newsroom.

Terry watched them as the approached his desk. "What's up detective?"

"This," Marshall stated as he placed a copy of the morning's paper on Terry's desk.

"I had nothing to do with that," Terry replied.

"It's okay, but it seems this killer has established some kind of connection with you, Marshall answered pointing to Terry. "So, we want to place a tap on your phone for the next time he calls. Maybe we'll be able to trace the call."

"Wait a minute," bellowed Fitch scurrying over to the copy desk. "Unless you have a warrant, we can't let you tap our phones. The First Amendment guarantees Freedom of the Press."

Marshall took a piece of paper from his jacket pocket. "First of all, this has nothing to do with Freedom of the Press. Second, here is your warrant."

Fitch grabbed the paper from Marshall's hand.

Marshall gave Fitch a few minutes to read the warrant. "Look all we want to do is tap Mr. Lambert's phone so that the next time the killer calls, we can get a trace on the call and record it. We're not interfering with your operation, nor are we trying to control what you print, *with the exception of anything about our investigation.* The less the killer knows about that, the better our chances of catching him."

"The public has a right to know what is going on," Fitch

stated. "It's our job to keep them informed and keep them out of danger."

"Normally, I would agree with you," Marshall replied. "But in this case, anything you print will inform the killer of our progress. We really don't want that. Also, it's obvious this individual has some kind of connection with Mr. Lambert. We want to keep the flow of information one way, from the killer to us, not the other way around."

"Is he in any danger?" Diana asked walking up to join the conversation.

Marshall turned to face her. "I doubt it. It seems the killer sees Mr. Lambert as a way to get the attention he wants. As long as Mr. Lambert and the paper give the killer the attention he wants, Mr. Lambert is in no danger."

"I don't know," Fitch said waving the warrant in his hand. "I'll have to check with our legal department about this."

"Well I do," Terry interjected. "Two women have died. This nut case is killing people and if there is anything I can do to stop it, I will. I don't care what the legal department says. Besides, most of my phone calls are from people in this office. Since everyone here knows what is going on, there really isn't any issue with protecting anyone's privacy."

"Hey, what if someone says something confidential?" Fitch asked.

Diana laughed. "With the amount of gossip going on in this place, nothing is confidential."

Marshall put up his hand to calm everyone down. "Look, we're not interested in office gossip. As for the warrant, it's legal, but go ahead and talk to your legal department. As for you Mr. Lambert, thank you for cooperating. Look on the bright side, if there is any danger, at least there will be a couple of cops here to take care of it."

"Just be sure to keep Terry safe," Diana added. "We're journalists and I know sometimes the job gets scary, but this is more than we need."

"Will do miss," Marshal answered.

Fitch stormed off to his office. Diana took a moment longer before returning to her desk. Marshall signaled to one of the individuals with him. "Mr. Lambert, this is Steven Cornell. He's the technician who will handle the phones for you. This other person is Detective David Freedman."

Detective Freedman stuck out his hand. "Pleased to meet you Mr. Lambert."

"Please, call me Terry."

"I'm Steven," the technician said as he shook Terry's hand. "If you let me in, I'll hook up your phone. It won't take but a couple of minutes. After that, if you have some place where I can set up, I'll be out of your way."

"Sure thing," Terry replied.

"By the way," Marshall said, "there will always be either myself or Detective Freedman here with Steven."

Terry smiled. "Even at night? I mean we are open from seven in the morning till about six. After that, everyone goes home."

"Do we need to provide security at night?" Freedman inquired.

Terry waved his hand. "I wouldn't think so. We have a night watchman. Besides, everything is locked up so no worries."

~ ~ ~

The rest of the day passed without incident. Marshall left, but Freedman stayed with Steven. Terry arranged for them to use a desk near his. While Terry worked, the two police officers passed their time cyber surfing and reading old newspapers. Whenever Terry's phone rang the two officers would quickly activate their system, only to be disappointed by the routine nature of the call. This continuing activity provided amusement for several of the reporters in the office. Once the paper's deadline passed, reporters finished up for the day.

Terry logged off his computer and turned to the two officers. "I hope today wasn't too much of a disappointment."

"Nah," answered Freedman. "Look at this way. It means we don't have another dead body."

"Yeah," Terry replied hoping to say something positive. "You know, some of us stop in at this bar, Murphy's, down the street for a drink after work. You're welcome to join us."

Freedman and Steven looked at each other. "Sure, why not," Steven replied.

Terry led the two officers to Murphy's. It was crowded with reporters telling stories or hoping to pick up on what others were working on. Fortunately, Terry and his guests were able to find a table. A young waitress came over and took their drink orders.

"Cheers," Terry said raising his glass of beer when their drinks arrived.

"Cheers," Freedman answered raising his Manhattan. Steven raised his glass of wine in a silent salute to both of them.

Terry took a long drink and set his glass down on the table. "I hope today wasn't too bad for you. I know it must be frustrating to sit around hoping he will call."

"It's not so bad," Freedman said. "It's a lot better than doing a stake out sitting in a car or an abandon building. Here we get to do something while waiting."

"He's right," Steven answered. "Normally, I have to sit in van and listen to tapes trying to figure out what they are really talking about. A lot of drug dealers and street thugs use a special code to make it harder for us, but we always figure it out."

"What are you talking about?" interrupted Ashford coming over uninvited. "Have you managed to catch the killer yet?"

"Who are you?" asked Freedman.

Terry picked up his beer and pointed to Ashford's general

direction. "Gentlemen, this is Ashford Zane. He's a reporter with The *City Times*. Ashford, meet Detective Freedman and Steven Cornell."

Ashford grunted a hello and nodded his head. "So, what are you doing now Runt? You think because you found a dead body you get to hang out with cops?"

Terry put down his beer. "Not that it's any of your concern, but I am helping Detective Freedman and Steven here with their investigation."

"Don't give me that," Ashford said with some irritation in his voice. "They're in the office tapping your phone, hoping the killer will call."

"Sir," Freedman said in a strong, quiet tone, "Please keep your voice down and the facts quiet. We really don't want others to know what we are doing."

"Freedom of the Press, brother," Ashford said waving his drink at Freedman. "We have Freedom of the Press, which means we can tell the public anything we want."

"No one is trying to stop Freedom of the Press," Terry replied. "What the detective is asking for you to lower your voice and not tell everyone about the investigation. Let's keep it a surprise until the killer is caught. After that, you can tell anyone and everyone. I'll even get you a bullhorn so that you can scream it in the streets."

"Listen Runt, I'll tell who ever I please, whenever I please." Before Terry could respond, Ashford left and returned to the bar. Terry and the two officers watched Ashford as he engaged in a conversation with several others at the bar.

"Maybe we should go over there and stop him," Terry suggested.

"Forget it," Freedman said. "It's too late. Everyone here heard what he said. Fortunately, beyond that, he doesn't know anything."

Chapter Six

Fitch was fuming when Terry walked in the next morning. "Will you look at this! We got scooped, and it's about our own reporters. How did they find out?"

Terry gave Fitch a confused look. "What are you talking about?"

"This," Fitch said thrusting a paper at Terry. "It's on the front page of another newspaper. We are helping the police and they are tapping our phones. Do you know what this does to our reputation?"

Terry took the paper from Fitch. The article explained in great detail the paper's involvement in the investigation, highlighting Terry's role. Terry returned the paper to Fitch. "I don't know where this information came from, but I certainly didn't tell anyone. Obviously, someone here is leaking the story to others."

"I think I know what happened," Ashford said coming up to join the conversation. "Last night Terry and the two cops were at Murphy's talking about the case. I'm sure someone overheard them and that's where the leak is."

"Bull," Terry replied. "The only one talking about the investigation was you. You were drunk and blabbed it to everyone in the bar."

"Don't be ridiculous," Ashford said waving his hand at Terry. "How would I know anything about the investigation? You're the one working with the police."

Before Terry could respond, Detective Marshall and Steven entered the office. Marshall was holding the same article Fitch had. "Who leaked this to the papers?"

"That's what we're trying to find out," Ashford replied. "The only one who really knows what's going on is Terry."

"I didn't tell anyone about the police being here or them tapping my phone," Terry vehemently denied, pointing to Ashford. "I'm willing to bet it was you and your big mouth yesterday at the bar."

"Hey, the last thing I would do is give a scoop to another newspaper."

Marshall threw the newspaper on a nearby desk. "Well someone had a big mouth. Now we're screwed. The killer is never going to call here again."

Terry's phone rang.

It rang again. Everyone in the room watched Terry as he walked over to pick up the receiver. "*City Times,* copy editing."

"Hello Terry," the voice at the other end said.

Terry placed the call on speaker. "Good to hear from you."

"You're lying, but that's okay. And I know you placed me on speaker. I can hear it on the phone. Well since everyone including the cops can hear me, just know I'm not through. I'll be in touch." The voice hung up.

"Great," Marshall shouted pounding a desk. "He calls and instead of getting the call on tape or a location, we're standing around here like a bunch of idiots."

"Personally, I don't care if we look stupid," Terry said. "What scares me is I know he is going to kill someone else, and we can't stop it."

~ ~ ~

Paula rarely read the newspaper. She found the news depressing, but the paper was free for customers at Le Rue. This morning it was different. She recognized the person on the front page. Paula had grabbed a sandwich at the deli counter in the corner supermarket for lunch. She managed to find an empty seat at Le Rue. She made sure no one wearing headphones was listening to music when she sat down. She unwrapped her sandwich and continued to read the paper.

"Paula, what a pleasant surprise."

Paula looked up and saw Ashford standing on the other side of the railing separating the dining area from pedestrian traffic.

"I met you a few days ago. You were here with a short guy, Terry."

"Oh yeah, now I remember you."

"Mind if I join you?"

Paula looked around to see if anyone was watching.

"Quit being so paranoid. I just wanted to say hello."

"Sorry," Paula said. "After what I read in the paper this morning, I want to be sure I'm not going to become another news story."

"Hey, I wouldn't do that to you. Do you mind if I joined you?"

"As long as you're not interviewing me."

"No, just looking for some company to share a cup of coffee with." Ashford went inside the café. He joined Paula a few minutes later.

"So, what's up?" Paula asked.

Ashford noticed the paper next to Paula. "I see you read our competitor's paper."

"It's free here. So is yours. I noticed the article on the front page. I know the guy." Paula said defensively.

"Relax, "Ashford said as he took a sip of his coffee. "I'm just making conversation. By the way, Terry is a really nice guy."

"Really, I didn't get the impression you two got along."

"Well we don't hang out together, but we work in the same office. When you work with someone every day, you kind of develop some sort of bond."

"Yeah, I know what you mean," said Paula taking a sip

of her coffee. "It was like that in the Marine Corps. In civilian life, you would have never associated with the person, but in the Corps, when you're in combat with him, you develop a bond. The longer you serve together, the stronger the bond becomes, regardless of any differences you have."

"Sounds like you miss the Marines."

"Some parts yes, other parts no."

"So why did you leave?"

Paula stared at Ashford. "It's not the kind of thing people want to talk about over coffee."

"Maybe we can talk about it some other time?"

Paula smiled. "No, I'm definitely not talking about my life to a reporter."

~ ~ ~

Joyce Youngblood enjoyed her time in the park. She loved being outside, which she attributed to her being one fourth Cherokee. She stopped by often to admire the flowers lining the pathways and the birds on the lake. She enjoyed watching children playing and people walking their dogs. For her, the park reaffirmed life.

"They really are interesting, aren't they?" someone said behind her. Joyce turned to see a man with a sparse beard, dressed in jeans and a yellow tee shirt. He pointed to the ducks on the lake. He had a package of crackers in one hand. He took one out and put it in his mouth. He held out the package to Joyce.

"No thank you," Joyce replied to the silent offering.

"What's wrong? Don't you want one? At least take one and feed it to the birds."

Joyce smiled at the man. "No, that's okay. It's really not a good idea to feed the birds. They become too dependent on people for food and they don't learn how to fend for themselves."

"Hogwash," the man said eating another cracker.

"They're birds. They'll always find bugs to eat."

Joyce smiled and turned to watch the birds on the lake.

"So, what brings you out here?" the man said quickly changing the subject.

"Just enjoying a day in the park. I like to get out and take in the fresh air. What about you?"

"Pretty much the same. I like the trees and flowers and stuff. It's better than being in an office all day."

"Well, I have to agree with you there. We really weren't made to work in an office all day."

"Is that what you do?" the man asked.

"Yeah, that's why I like coming here. Four walls with a window isn't the same as walking through grass and feeling fresh air."

"Couldn't agree with you more. You've got to take the small pleasures in life."

"Yes, that's true. Well, I've got to get back to work. You take care." Joyce gave the man a small wave as she walked away."

The man watched her walking away, knowing she would never leave the park.

Chapter Seven

Terry arrived early the next day. "What should I do?" he asked the photo of the attractive brunette on his desk while taking a sip of coffee. "Every day I hope he will call. I want to hear from him. I hope each time he calls he will leave some clue so that we can catch him. But each time he calls, it means an innocent girl has been killed." Terry put Kristen's photo back in its place.

"How many cups of coffee have you had?" Diana asked as she walked in and put her purse down.

"Three. Why?"

"Normally, you're half asleep until ten when the foreign press stories start to arrive. But this morning, you're talking to Kristen's photo and you can't sit still. Either you are very excited, or you have ants in your pants."

"Probably the ants," answered Ashford walking in.

Diana went over to the coffee pot and poured herself a cup. "Ashford, you really do like to make an entrance, don't you?"

Ashford spread his arms out wide. "Hey, I'm here, I'm here. Let the banners fly and the trumpet blare. I'm here I'm here."

"Isn't that from a Bugs Bunny cartoon?" Terry commented.

"So what?" Ashford retorted.

"Now, now boys, play nice," Diana interrupted.

"Morning," Detective Freedman said as he and Steven Cornell came into the office. "I was going to offer you a cup of coffee, but I see you already have one," he said to Terry.

"Thanks. Appreciate the consideration," Terry replied.

Steven set a box of donuts and a large carton of coffee on the desk next to Terry. He opened the box and took one out. "Then how about a donut?"

Terry smiled. "I guess it's true what they say about cops and donuts. You have to have them to start your day."

"Breakfast of champions," Steven said with a mouthful of a chocolate-covered confectionary.

"Aw great, donuts," Ashford cried out, grabbing two of them before moving onto his desk. "Has the dingbat called yet?"

Terry whispered to the detective. "No, he just walked into the office a few minutes ago." Both officers snickered. Even Diana smiled at the comment as she took a donut.

The mood was shattered with the ringing of the phone. Terry took a deep breath, and let it ring a second time before picking up the receiver. "*City Times*, copy desk, how can I help you?"

"You don't sound very happy to hear from me," the voice said.

Terry could imagine the person at the other end gleefully smiling. Terry turned and saw Steven had already started the trace. "Well, we always appreciate you calling and telling us about your stories. Do you have anything interesting for us today?"

"Listen Terry," the voice said. "I really don't have much time. I know the police are trying to trace this call, but it won't do them any good. Your next story is in East Lake Park. Don't forget to feed the ducks." The voice laughed before hanging up.

Terry hung up the phone. "Did you get a trace?" He demanded.

Steve held up his hand as he pushed some buttons. After a minute he turned off the machine "No," Steven said with disappointment. "He knew not to stay on the line very long.

He used a cell phone and he's taken out the sim card or somehow disabled it. The closest we have to a location is triangulation of the signal. It's in the park he just mentioned on the phone."

Detective Freedman pushed speed dial on his cell phone. "We got another body. It's in East Lake Park, but we've got to find it."

Terry, along with Detective Freedman and Steven, rushed out of the office. The ride from the newspaper office to the park took less than ten minutes. By the time they arrived, there were more than a dozen police cars and several teams of officers searching the area.

"He said to be sure to feed the ducks," Terry said running up to Detective Marshall. "I think we should look by the pond."

"Already have people doing that," Marshall replied.

"Anything we can do?" Freedman asked.

"Yes," Terry shouted. "I haven't been here for a long time, but I just remembered there used to be an aviary where they kept injured birds. Kids often got to feed them, especially the ducks and geese that were hurt."

"Pretty crappy place to put a body," Marshall said. "Some kids might find the body."

"Except the place doesn't open for another hour," Terry said. "It would be a great place to put the body, and make sure it wouldn't be found until we got here."

Marshall and the others hurried to the aviary and found it locked. Freedman took out his cell phone and called the desk sergeant to get someone to open the place. While they were waiting at the entrance, Terry started walking along the fence. Less than fifty feet from the entrance, hidden behind a large bush, he found a section of fence that had been cut away.

"Hey, I found a way in" Terry called to the others. He didn't wait. He entered the compound. Marshall,

Freedman, and Steven soon joined Terry. Terry and Marshall went to the right of opening while the other two went to the left. Walking through the bushes and the trees made it difficult to make much progress or to see farther than a few feet. It didn't matter. It took Terry and Marshal only a few minutes before the came to the edge of a small man-made stream and the body of a young woman.

~ ~ ~

He was eating a donut when Terry and two others arrived at the park. He couldn't take a chance that the dwarf would recognize him from the fairgrounds, so he stayed in his truck and watch through binoculars. He knew most criminals were caught because they made mistakes in thinking the cops would never connect them to the crime. He wasn't going to let that happen. He would have to be satisfied with watching them from a distance. He grinned when he saw the cops and Terry head towards the ariary. He knew he wouldn't see much, but he would wait, at least until the coroner arrived.

~ ~ ~

Terry hoped the plaster would wash off his shoes. The crime scene technician said it would when she took plaster casts of his footprints to eliminate his footprints from ones possibly made by the killer at the scene. Terry didn't see the need for this because his feet were smaller than anyone else's.

He was back in the office, at his desk. He took out his notebook. The third victim was Joyce Youngblood. She had been stabbed twice, just like the second victim. Her body had been hidden from view. All three victims were young women in their mid-twenties, single, fairly attractive, and residents of the city.

Terry started his article, knowing he would have to wait for more details from the police, which they promised to have for him by this afternoon. Terry pondered over each word, every sentenced, every period and comma. He sat in his chair, his body leaning to one side, but he didn't care. He thought he would be happy to be writing news again. Instead he felt a dull ache in his chest, realizing young women had to die for him to have a story. Terry was finding that he liked his job of simply editing stories written by others a lot more satisfying than this assignment. He reached for Kristen's photo, hoping she could give him some kind of guidance.

The phone rang. Terry absent-mindedly reached for it, stopping before his hand touched the instrument. It rang for a second time. Terry slowly picked it up. "*City Times*, copy editing."

"You don't sound too happy." Terry cringed. It was the voice again. "I heard on the news you found my gift to you."

Terry turned around to stare at the empty place where Steven should be to record and trace the phone call. Frustration seized Terry because he did not know how to turn on the machine setting on the desk behind him. Desperately he looked to see if he could find the switch to activate the machine.

"Terry," the voice said in a melodic tone. "Are you upset with me?"

Terry angrily turned back to his desk and grabbed a pen and paper. "Of course I'm upset. You're killing innocent girls. Why are you doing this?"

"Who said they were innocent? Besides, your job is to print the story; not to question me. You wouldn't want me to stop calling you and call someone else instead, would you?"

"No, no," Terry forcefully said into the phone, attracting the attention of many of those in the newsroom. Several of the reporters left their desks and drifted toward Terry. Terry became aware of them, but he forced himself to calm down and concentrate on the phone call.

"Good," the voice continued. "I think it's time I made a statement to the press."

"Certainly," Terry answered, still holding a pen over a sheet of paper. "Give it to me and I'll write it down."

The voice laughed. "Do you think I'm stupid? I'm not staying on the phone long enough for you to trace this call. Go to the main library. I hope you're a mystery fan. I'm partial to Sherlock Holmes. Good bye Terry." The voice hung up.

Terry slammed down the receiver of his phone. He rubbed his face several times before looking up and seeing several reporters staring at him.

"That was the killer, wasn't it?" Wanda Terrell, the science and lifestyle reporters asked.

"Yeah, it was him," Terry answered.

"What did he say?" asked Diana coming over to Terry's desk.

"He said..." Terry stopped himself from completing the sentence. "I think maybe I should talk to the police before I say anything else."

"Of course," Diana agreed. "Is there anything we can do to help?"

"Yes," Terry said excitedly. "I have to go and take care of something. If I could get Carl to finish up editing today's copy; that would be helpful."

"You got it," Carl answered.

Terry jumped off his chair and grabbed his coat. "As for the rest of you, help Carl out and double check your copy before turning it in. Tell Fitch I'll be back as soon as I can."

Terry ran out of the building. He also literally ran into Paula, knocking her and himself off their feet.

"Whoa guy. We have to stop meeting like this. Not only are people beginning to talk, but it's getting hard on the bones."

"Sorry," Terry said smiling at Paula while getting up.

"I'm in a bit of a hurry."

Paula stood up and brushed herself off. "I should hope so. I would hate to think you were waiting until I came along before ambushing me."

"I'm sorry, but I really need to be somewhere," Terry said finishing his sentence, holding up his hand for a taxi, which pulled to the curb.

"Yeah, I understand," Paula said grinning, brushing herself off. "Hot scoop and you've got to get there first. You have deadlines before the presses can roll and all that stuff."

"Right," Terry said over his shoulder as he jumped in the taxi.

~ ~ ~

The main library had taken its look from the New York Public Library, complete with the statues of two lions in front. The first floor was modern with the reception desk, computers, reading rooms, and periodicals. Terry had to go to the third floor to find the mystery novels. He carefully searched the entire section, looking for another body or clue to where it was. He found himself staring at dozens of mystery novels. Terry started pulling the books off the shelves and looking through them. When he pulled the novel *The Adventures of Sherlock Holmes*, a single piece of paper floated to the ground. Terry picked it up and unfolded it.

There are too many people who feel they are better than others simply because they were born to wealth or beauty. These people who don't do any work look down on the working class, the true heroes of America. It is time for those who treat the working class with disrespect and no appreciation to learn their real place in society.

The game is afoot. Hope you are ready for an adventure Terry. Here is your first clue – members of the royal court need to remember their subjects are just as important as they are.

Great, thought Terry. This guy really is delusional.

~ ~ ~

"What are you doing here?" Ashford demanded when Terry entered the police station briefing room. "I'm covering the story. You can go back to the paper."

"Ashford, I'm not in the mood," Terry answered as he pushed pass Ashford. "Where are the detectives?"

Ashford grabbed Terry's coat and pushed him up against a wall. "Listen Runt. If you got something about the case, you need to give it to me, and I mean right now."

Terry squirmed and managed to free himself from Ashford's grasp. "Don't do that. And I don't have to give you anything. And for your information, I'm covering the story."

Ashford leaned over Terry. "Don't get snippy with me Runt. I'll get you fired. The brass listens to me."

"They have no choice. You're like a foghorn, really hard to ignore. Now, get out of my way." Terry pushed himself away from Ashford and walked up to an officer standing by a door. After a brief conversation, the officer led Terry into another room. Ashford watched and wrote something in his notebook.

The officer took Terry to the detective squad room, where he found Detectives Marshall and Freedman.

"What's up," Freedman asked.

Terry handed Freedman the paper he had taken from the library. "I got a call from the killer when I got back to the office. He told me to go to the library. I thought maybe there was another victim, but instead I found this."

"Wish you had left it there," Freedman said, taking a nitrile glove from a box on his desk and wrapping it around the edge of the paper as he took it from Terry. "It would have been useful to have the lab techs to go over the scene."

"I can take you back to where I got the note."

Freedman signaled for Steven to come over. "Why don't you go with Mr. Lambert here and see if you can get anything from the scene. Did you find anything else?"

Terry sheepishly looked down at the ground. "I didn't check. Once I found that, I came directly here."

Steven grabbed his portable crime scene kit. "Let's go back and take another look. We probably won't find anything, but we need to check it out to be sure."

Terry was grateful he didn't run into Ashford when he and Steven left the detectives. They got into Steven's car to return to the library.

~ ~ ~

He laughed when Terry ran into that tall blond. He watched as Terry got up and into a taxi. He put his pickup into gear and followed the taxi,

The man had to find a parking space before he could follow Terry into the library. He made sure to put on a baseball hat and a large jacket to hide his frame and face from any cameras in the building. From a distance, he pretended to look for a book while watching Terry frantically searching. He giggled when Terry started going through the mystery books. He hoped he could be patient till Terry found the note. Terry did. Terry grabbed the note and ran out the door. He knew where Terry was going, and he knew Terry would return.

He didn't have long to wait. He crackled with joy as he watched the scene at the library. The police were there with their yellow tapes, and bystanders intently watched while the police dusted for prints and looked for clues. They wouldn't find any. He had been careful. He had worn gloves when producing the note and when he planted it in the mystery section of the library. His only worry was what if someone had checked out the book before that reporter found it. That's why he planted the note that morning. He wasn't worried about appearing on any surveillance camera. After all, there were dozens of people visiting the library, and the police had no idea what he looked like. Here he was, less than twenty yards from them and not one of them knew. Still, he made it a point to stay in the back of the crowd and away from the dwarf. He didn't want Terry to see him.

~ ~ ~

Terry was uncomfortable standing in the library while Steven examined the books in the mystery section. Steven collected latent prints, mostly partials and smudges, from the shelves and books. It took Steven almost two hours to collect and photograph all the prints; during which time a crowd of patrons had gathered to watch. Steven often smiled and nodded to those watching while Terry nervously paced around the area. Steven had given Terry the job of keeping the bystanders at bay.

"What's going on?" was the question continuously being asked. Terry, afraid of compromising the investigation, gave a vague answer stating Steven was lifting some prints, but he couldn't comment on the investigation. Several of the bystanders took photographs of Steven working with their cell phones. Terry now realized how uncomfortable it made others when reporters took photographs without asking those being photographed. One reporter even tried to get a statement from Terry for a television news report. Ashford was in the crowd and he made sure Terry saw him. He even took a picture of Terry standing behind the yellow crime scene tape. Steven finished, cleaned up, and motioned for Terry it was time to leave. Terry rushed through the onlookers, only to have to wait for Steven as he made his way through the group, stopping to smile and briefly chat with a couple of attractive young ladies. Terry's anxiety increased when he saw Ashford smiling from the back of the group. Terry was glad when they left to return to the police station.

"So now that you have the killer's fingerprints, you can identify him and arrest him."

Steven smiled before answering. "Real life is nothing like it is on TV."

"Of course not," Terry agreed. "Television is for entertainment; it's fiction. That stuff isn't real."

"Well, the science in the program is real," Steven stated. "What isn't real is the situation. Most of the time we get partials or smudges, which aren't conclusive. We rarely find a fingerprint that leads us to a killer. Even if we do find a fingerprint, all it proves is the person was there. It was a public library, so it's hardly incriminating. Also, the fingerprints we find aren't always in the system. Not everyone has been fingerprinted."

"So, it was pretty much a waste of time," Terry said disappointedly.

"No, it wasn't. One the important things is to collect evidence for court. It's doubtful anything today will help us identify the killer; but it might help us get a conviction when we do arrest him and take him to trial. The goal isn't just to catch the bad guys; it's to put them away so they can't hurt anyone else."

"So, what do we do next?" Terry asked.

"I'll run the prints through our databases and hopefully come up with something. You go back to your office and wait for him to call again."

"Okay," Terry replied, "I have to go back anyway to write about this third murder. But you need to show me how to turn on the machine, so I can trace the call if you're not there when he calls again."

~ ~ ~

He glanced at the clock and realized the news was coming on. He grabbed the control and turned on the TV. When the anchor person led the news with a report about the police finding the note, he jumped up and down on his couch. They called him the "Sherlock Holmes Killer." He liked that. The reporter talked about the case, and the discovery of the note in the novel. Then he saw the reporter try interviewing Terry.

"Terry," he said in a sing-song voice. "Don't get angry. We are just beginning a new game, and it's going to be a lot of fun."

Chapter Eight

The next morning, Terry was again greeted by an unwelcomed headline as he entered the office. This time there was no question about where it came from. It had Ashford's byline. Across the top banner was the headline "Sherlock Holmes Killer Strikes Again." Terry grabbed a copy of the paper and stormed into Fitch's office.

"What's going on," Terry demanded thrusting the paper at Fitch. "I'm supposed to write the stories, not Ashford. Why is Ashford writing about this case? What happened to the story I wrote? And the information about the note in a Sherlock Holmes novel was supposed to be a secret. We can't print everything. We can't tell the killer everything we know. If we do, we'll never catch him."

"What's this *we* stuff?" Fitch asked. "We're a newspaper. Our job is to publish the news, not catch criminals. It's the police's job to get this guy. You don't think this guy knows the note he planted was in a Sherlock Holmes novel. He put it there. Furthermore, it was the lead story of almost every local TV station in the city. It's not a secret, Trust me."

"But we should focus our efforts on helping the police, not giving this guy publicity."

"Terry, if we don't give him the publicity he craves, he'll go to another paper. He will keep killing. That won't stop. Giving him publicity isn't encouraging him to kill others. It might even give him what he wants, and he'll slow down or stop."

Terry yanked the paper off of Fitch's desk. "No, it won't. He wants attention, and the more we give him, the more he will want. And that means the more women he will kill."

"You're probably right."

"And what happened to the story I wrote? Why is Ashford's in the paper and not mine?"

"Ashford got his in first, so it got laid in. Your story didn't add anything, and it left out the part about the note, so we kept Ashford's."

Terry returned to his desk. He saw Ashford smiling, which only added to his anger.

~ ~ ~

Once again, Paula treated herself to overpriced coffee at Le Rue. *Dumb, really dumb* Paula said to herself reading the front page of the *City Times*. It didn't help that the story made the evening news the night before. The police were going to be swamped with kooks claiming they were the killer, hoping to get attention. By releasing everything to the media, it would make it harder to eliminate the nuts cases from the real killer, if he decided to come in and confess. The chances of that were limited. The killer would get a lot more of the attention he craved from continuing his crime spree than from confessing. Still, it was dumb to tell the public everything the police knew to the killer.

"I see you're a fan of our newspaper."

Paula looked up and saw Diana. "What can I do for you?" Paula asked. As soon as she said it she realized she was being blunt and defensive.

"Nothing," Diana replied. "Just saw you and thought I would say hi. Which story are you reading?"

"Excuse me, but who are you?"

"I tried to interview you for a story. I'm a reporter for the paper you're reading. So are you reading my story, or someone else's?"

Paula folded the newspaper so that the headline was clearly visible. "This one, the one about the killer and his games with the police."

"You're not afraid, are you?"

"No, it's just that I thought a reporter named Terry was covering the story; but I see this Ashford Zane writing about it?"

"So, you're familiar with some of our reporters," Diana stated with mild surprise.

"Not really. I've ran into Terry a couple of times, and I've met Ashford."

"I didn't know you were friends with Terry."

"Why?" Paula demanded. "Would that surprise you? Terry and someone like me, tall and big boned?"

"No. Terry's a really nice guy. I want to see him get out and be with others."

"Quit trying to fix me up," Paula said with a smile. "I think he's nice, but he's not my type."

"Why, because he's a dwarf?"

"No, his size isn't the issue. I'm just not in a place right now where I can handle any kind of relationship."

"Well, if that changes…"

"Hey, if Terry is such a nice guy, why aren't you dating him?"

"It's hard to explain. I work with him. I knew his wife. He's a dear friend and I do care about him. But he's still in love with his wife."

"What happened? They get divorced?"

"Wish it were that simple. He might be able to move on if that were the case."

"So, what did happen?"

"That's something I think Terry should tell you. I can tell you that he still cares about her, even though she's been gone for more than four years."

"I can understand that," Paula replied. "When I was in the Corps, there were guys I would go to the ends of the earth for. They were brothers. We fought and lived together. You only had to call, and we would be there for each other.

We loved each other. We would get drunk together, party together, do wild and crazy things together. They're gone. Some of them got out. Some of them didn't make it back. Doesn't matter. They become part of you and you can't let go."

"You miss the Corps, don't you?"

"Yeah, in a way, I do. But in a way, I can never go back. I was proud and honored to serve. But I need to put it behind me and move on."

"That's why you didn't want me to do a story about you."

Paula leaned back in her chair and stared at Diana. "For some veterans, their service is full of stories they like to tell at bars for free beer. For many others, it's things they've discovered about themselves they wish they had never known. A lot of people lost their humanity over there, and they're afraid they will never get it back. Killing people is not something anyone should be proud of. Let's change the subject. What can you tell me about this story and the killer?"

"Nothing really. He's called the paper a couple of times, and Terry answered the phone. He's using Terry to get publicity in the paper."

Paula put down her cup of coffee. "This guy's killed three women. He's not going to have any trouble getting the attention he craves. He no longer needs the paper for publicity, so tell Terry to be careful. This guy is mentally unbalanced, which means he could come after Terry, or anyone else associated with the story, at any minute, for any or no reason. Don't be fooled into looking for some kind of psychological motive. He's learned to kill, and he likes it."

"What makes you so sure?"

"I've seen it too many times when I was in Iraq. There were those who enjoyed the killing. They would make up some excuse such as they are fighting for a cause; but the truth was they were evil, and they enjoyed hurting others."

Paula stood up and left before Diana could respond.

~ ~ ~

Detectives Marshall and Freedman, along with Steven, entered the pressroom. Steven went immediately to the machine he had set up. Freedman calmly took off his coat, folded it neatly, and placed on the back of a chair. Marshall stood there with his hands on his hip, looking around the pressroom. He stopped when his gaze landed on Ashford. Marshall continued to stare at Ashford. Soon all the others were staring too.

"What is your problem?" Ashford demanded.

"You," was Marshall's answer.

Ashford looked around the room. He picked up some papers from his desk, briefly looked at them, before throwing them down on his desk. Marshall continued staring at him.

"What?" Ashford loudly demanded. "Why are you staring at me? I haven't done anything wrong."

Probably because he has never seen a jackass wearing pants thought Terry.

"You wrote about the note being found in the library," Marshall stated. "Because of your arrogance, the media and the killer now know everything we know. So does every nut job coming in to confess to these killings, hoping to get their names in the paper. There are things we like to keep secret; but you had to tell all. Keeping details secret helps us determine any lies a suspect might tell us."

"It's called *Freedom of the Press*," Ashford forcefully said. "The public has a right to know."

"Don't give me that crap," Marshall answered with anger in his voice. "You care about as much as a turnip about the public. Your stunt told the killer we knew about the library and that he left notes there. That means he won't go back and that makes it much harder to catch him."

"He was never going back," Ashford said interrupting

73

the detective. "He knows Terry tells you everything. It was a one-time deal, so you had nothing to lose. Besides with the crowd you were drawing there yesterday, he probably saw what you were doing. I'll bet you it's even on Facebook."

"He wasn't there," Terry said. "If he had shown up, I would have seen him."

"You know what the killer looks like?" Diana asked.

"No, he doesn't," Ashford replied. "He saw someone once at the fairgrounds and he gave the police a description. But he really hasn't seen the killer."

"Quiet Ashford," Diana demanded. "Seriously, Terry do you know what the killer looks like?"

"Who told you about Mr. Lambert's description?" Marshall asked Ashford.

"I'm a reporter. I have my sources. I know all he saw was someone at the fairgrounds who gave him a hard time. But he didn't see the killer."

Terry pointed at Ashford. "I'm telling you I saw the killer. I'm sure he was the person who was hassling me and the victim at the fairgrounds the night she was murdered. It's only a matter of time before I can prove it."

"Whoa, whoa, whoa," Marshall said holding up his hands to calm everyone down. He looked around the room, making eye contact with each individual. He pointed to Fitch. "You, you're the editor, so you will make sure nothing else gets printed about this case without clearing it with us first. Whatever you do, don't print anything about the person Terry saw at the fairgrounds. We don't know if that person is the killer or not. Leave the police work to us. Of course, we want Terry to maintain his connection with the killer; but Terry doesn't have to prove anything to anyone. As for the rest of you, go about your business and leave the police work to us. And please don't write any stories about what we are doing. Let's quit tipping off the killer about our every move."

"This is my paper, and you don't get to tell me what to do," Fitch yelled. "Ashford's right. It's *Freedom of the Press*, and you can't stop it."

Marshall walked up to Fitch. "Look, we really need each other, not only for this case, but for every other case we have to deal with. Either we work together and cooperate on this, or I will see to it that your *newspaper* is always a day late and a dollar short for every crime story in this city for the next decade. Let's face it, working together benefits both of us."

Fitch pointed his finger at Marshall. "Just remember, we're doing you a favor, and you owe us. Don't forget that."

"Oh, I won't forget what you're doing. I can promise that."

Fitch returned to his office. The reporters slowly returned to their desks.

"I'm sorry about all this," Terry said to Marshall. "I should have known Ashford would do something like this when I saw him at the library yesterday."

"Don't worry about it," Steven said patting Terry on the arm. "I doubt the perpetrator will return to the library. He knows we'll staked it out in case he does. Not that it helps. We really don't know who we are looking for. We can't arrest everyone who checks out a mystery novel."

"What about my description?"

"Well, we can stop those who fit the description, but all we have is a person who was at the fairgrounds the night of a murder. There were thousands there, so it really doesn't prove anything."

"So, what should we do?"

"Truthfully, there is little we can do except wait. The next move is up to him."

Chapter Nine

Paula walked around her car examining the repair job to the fender. "It looks like new. You really do great work."

"Aw, this was easy," Ed said. "I was able to get the fender and headlight from a junk yard. It was the same make and model as yours. All I really had to do was match the paint job, which wasn't that hard because it was same color as yours. I just had to touch it up a bit. You want to know the best part?"

"What?"

"The whole thing, the fender, the paint, the labor, is less than two hundred dollars."

That was great news to Paula and her wallet. "Can I pay with a credit card?"

"Hey, it's the 21st Century. Of course, you can use a credit card."

Paula gave Ed her credit card and followed him into his office. Ed ran the card through the scanner while Paula busied herself looking at various fliers and posters on the wall.

"Just sign here," Ed said handing Paula a small clipboard with the receipt on it.

Paula signed the receipt and handed back to Ed. "By the way, what did you do with the old fender?"

"It's out back. I kept the old parts and turn them in for scrap metal about every three months or so. Why? Did you want it back?"

"Oh no," Paula answered. "Just curious. Do you mind if I look back there?"

"No, not all. But be careful. I wouldn't want you to fall and get hurt."

Ed watched Paula as she rounded the corner of the building, staying on a path through the grass and weeds. He kept watching, waiting for her to return. After several minutes he started around the building. "Miss, you okay?" he called out."

"I'm fine," Paula said as she came around the corner of the building.

"What were you looking for?"

"I wanted to see if there were any parts of a blue pickup truck back there."

"I don't think so," Ed said rubbing his chin. "Why?"

"I think it was a blue pickup that hit my car. If he got his truck fixed here, then I could find out who the driver was."

Ed let out a small laugh. "Well I can tell you I haven't worked on any blue pickup trucks lately. But even if I had, I couldn't give you the driver's name. That's considered private information and I can get into a lot of trouble giving it out."

"Well, it was worth a shot."

"What part of the pickup hit your car?"

"I don't know. When I got back to my car that night, I found the fender and headlight smashed. A blue pickup almost ran me down a few minutes earlier. I'm not sure it was the same car that smashed into mine, but it's a place to start looking."

"Sorry I can't help you."

Paula gave Ed a smile. "Actually, you have."

~ ~ ~

For two days Terry jumped each time his phone rang. He dreaded answering it, fearing the voice would be at the other end. Ashford made it a point to call Terry several times on the phone instead of simply walking over to ask a question about grammar or spelling. Several other reporters commented on his behavior. Ashford didn't seem to care; he kept calling.

The phone rang. Terry glared at Ashford. He was tired of Ashford's games. Terry's anger dissipated when saw Ashford was typing on his computer and not using his phone. Terry turned to Steven who started his machine. "Good afternoon. *City Times*, copy editing,"

"Hello, Terry." It was the voice.

Terry took a deep breath and let it out slowly. "Hello yourself. Where have you been? Kind of hoping you were taking a vacation or something."

"Now Terry, don't be that way. You know I have a story for you. Don't you want it?"

Terry looked over at Steven who kept rolling his hand in a circle, signaling for Terry to keep the other person on the line. Terry took another deep breath and slowly let it out. "I don't know. Does it involve the murder of an innocent girl?"

"Hey, I know what makes headlines and what doesn't"

"Look, you don't have to do this," Terry pleaded. He took another deep breath. "There are other ways to get news coverage. If you talk to me, I'm sure I can help you."

"You think I'm a fool," the voice yelled. "I know you are dragging this out so that the police can trace the call. Well, I don't care. But you need to listen because I'm only going to tell you once. You sound like you need to get some exercise."

"What would you suggest? Maybe I should take up jogging in the park?'

"Nah. The fresh air will do you good, but what you really need is to join a gym. Hope you find a good one. The voice laughed.

"You still there?" Terry asked, getting no answer. He turned to face Steven.

Steven signaled for Terry to continue.

"Hello, hello," Terry yelled into the phone, still getting no answer.

"I got it," Steven exclaimed, "the call is coming from an address a few blocks from here." Steven showed Terry the address.

"That's Paula's gym," Terry yelled. "We've got to get there to save her."

Freedman, who was in the office, grabbed a hand-held radio. "Dispatch. Send two units and a backup detective squad to the gym located in the 4200 block of Broad Street. Possible homicide."

Everyone stopped and watched as the police officers rushed out. For a few seconds, Terry sat there with phone in his hand. Suddenly, he slammed the receiver down and ran out of the office.

~ ~ ~

All the participants were happy – the class was finished. Once again, they had survived thirty minutes of aerobic exercise. They congratulated themselves as they wiped the sweat from the faces and bodies before going to the locker room or leaving the gym. Paula started putting away the music and weights she had used in class. As she placed the weights on the racks, she noticed the man next to the phone at the receptionist's desk. He was medium height and weight. He looked out of place, being in street clothes. Paula assumed he had come in for information or some other benign reason. What puzzled her was the Kelly, the receptionist wasn't at the counter. She's probably using the bathroom or getting something from the office Paula thought as the man left the building. Paula returned to arranging the room. She was almost finished when two men with pistols burst through the door.

Paula picked up a five-pound flat weight and flung it at the first man, hitting him in the arm. The second individual turned and leveled his weapon at her. Paula was already running to the door at the other side of the room, keeping a wall between her and the man with the gun. The individual could see Paula running because of the mirrors on the opposite wall. He ran to cut her off at the door. Paula reached the door and waited. When she saw the door begin to open, she kicked it, knocking the individual flat on his back. He still had the weapon in his hand. Paula stomped on it, forcing him to let go of it. She bent down to pick up weapon when she heard "Stop! Police!"

Paula slowly stood up and raised her hands to face the individual she had hit with the weight. "If you're cops, show me your ID." As soon as she said it, she realized it was a foolish thing to say. If they weren't cops, they would shoot her. Three ladies came out of the women's locker room and screamed when they saw the man with a gun pointed at Paula.

"Police," he shouted as he pulled out a badge.

"That's right lady," said the individual laying on the floor at Paula's feet. "We're cops. Now get off of my hand."

Paula stepped back and allowed the individual to get up.

"I'm Detective Freedman and that's Officer Steven Cornell. We're looking for a man. He would have been using your phone just before we got here."

"You missed him by about five minutes," Paula stated. "There was someone here, but he's gone."

"And who are you?" demanded Freedman.

"Paula Stanford. I'm one of the instructors here. I just finished a class. If you don't believe me, you can ask those three over there. They were in the class."

"That's right," exclaimed one of the ladies. "We were in her class."

Steven holstered his weapon. "Did anyone see a man using the phone?" The three ladies all shook their head no.

"I saw a guy out here when I was putting away the equipment," Paula said. "He was hanging around the receptionist's desk."

"Can you describe him?" asked Freedman.

"Average height, medium build, Caucasian, about thirty something, and he had a bit of beard, not much, more of a fuzzy face than anything."

"Would you recognize him if you saw him again?"

Before Paula could answer, Terry ran into the room, breathing heavily. "Did you guys get him?"

"Oh my goodness," one of the three women exclaimed. "Is there a criminal here? Is he a murderer or a rapist? Are we safe?"

"Calm down ladies," Freedman replied. "He's gone and you're safe. Since you didn't see anything, why don't you give Officer Cornell your names and contact information. If we need anything else from you, we'll call."

Seeing everyone was alive, Terry leaned back on the reception counter breathing heavily. "You didn't get him? He was here, wasn't he?"

"Looks that way," Freedman answered. "I should arrest you for assault," he said to Paula.

"Nice try, but I saw two men with guns. I'm not some damsel who goes into distress every time there's danger. I fight back."

Terry, still breathing heavily asked. "Are you here alone?"

"No, Kelly's here. She's the receptionist."

"Where is she?" Freedman asked.

Paula rushed pass everyone and ran into the office behind the counter. Kelly was on the floor. From the blood pooling around her, Paula knew she was dead.

~ ~ ~

"Give me another," Paula demanded, banging her glass on bar counter.

"Don't you think you should slow down?"

Paula looked around to see who was questioning her.

Terry held up his hand and waved hi. "I watched you when you left. Sorry about your friend."

The bartender had refilled her drink. She grabbed hold of it, then turned to Terry. "You want one?"

Terry climbed up on a bar stool next to Paula. "Sure." The bartender automatically put down a shot glass and filled it from the bottle of Jim Beam Paula had been drinking. "What was your friend's name?"

"Kelly, Kelly Richards."

"To Kelly Richards."

"To Kelly."

Paula and Terry drained their glasses in a single gulp.

"You want to tell me about her?" Terry asked.

Paula signaled for the bartender to refill their glasses. "No, I don't. I don't want her life to be tomorrow's headlines. She deserves better than that."

Terry toyed with his drink. "You're right. She does. But she will be. I kind of would like for people to know what kind of person she was. I don't want people to see her as the fourth victim. I want people to see her as a person who was brutally murdered. Someone who had a life, dreams, friends, hope..."

"You want to sell headlines; don't lie to me."

"Don't" Terry demanded.

Paula drained her drink. "Don't what."

"Don't define me by some arbitrary standard you have created. People have done that my entire life. 'You're a dwarf. You should be a clown.' Well, I'm not. I'm a person. I might be extremely short, but I have all of the abilities and desires that everyone else possesses. And don't think I haven't experienced what you are going through. How do you think I felt when the police told me about my wife, the woman who I loved, had been killed in a senseless traffic accident? I do know and understand how you feel."

"You never told me your wife was killed."

"It's not something I like to discuss. It was a terrible time for me, so I really do know what you are going through."

"Sorry for your loss. Still, you're a reporter."

"No, I'm a person who writes the news and somehow got mixed up with a serial killer. It makes me sick. Every time my phones rings, I cringed. I'm afraid it will be him telling me about another innocent girl he has murdered. I just wish there was some way I could help the police catch him."

Paula turned to stare at Terry. "Do you really mean that?"

"Of course."

"Then we need to talk."

"How much have you had to drink?"

"Not enough," was Paula's answer as she grabbed the bottle of Jim Beam off the bar.

Paula's apartment was simple. It had a single bedroom off of a large room that served as the kitchen, dining room and living room combined. She had a kitchen table with four chairs, decorated with only a set of salt and pepper shakers. There was a single picture of a beach with sailboats on her wall. Terry sat on the second-hand couch while Paula made coffee in the kitchen area. On a bookcase were several pictures of groups of Marines in desert uniforms.

"You take milk or sugar?" she asked as she poured the dark brown liquid into two mismatched mugs.

"No, I drink it black," Terry answered.

"Good, because I don't have either one." Paula set the mugs down on the military food locker she used as a coffee table in front of Terry. She pulled another bottle of whiskey from a cupboard and pour some in here coffee. "Want some?'

"No thanks. Don't think you should finish one bottle before starting another one," Terry said pointing to the bottle she had brought from the bar.

"Don't worry, I will. Now, tell me what you know about

this guy who keeps calling you."

"Nothing."

"What do you mean?"

Terry took a sip of coffee. It was strong and bitter. "What kind of coffee is this?"

"It's from Saudi Arabia. It might be a bit strong for you. I developed a taste for it when I was in Iraq."

"I'm beginning to regret not following your example and lacing it with whiskey."

"The offer still stands," Paula said holding up a bottle. "Now quite trying to change the subject and tell me what you know about the killer."

"He's crazy. He's psychopath."

"What about his voice?"

"He uses a machine; it distorts his voice. It sounds like a cross between Darth Vadar and Donald Duck."

"How long does he stay on the line?"

"Less than a minute, not even thirty seconds. He intentionally keeps it short so that the police can't trace the call. Today was the first time he stayed on the line long enough for a trace. But he wanted it that way. He wanted the police to go to the gym and find your friend."

"What do you know about the victims?"

Terry gave Paula a confused look. "Nothing. I don't know any of them."

Paula put her cup on the table between them. "Do they look the same, are they the same age, same color hair, etc."

Terry held up his finger to signal he needed a minute to collect his thoughts. "They were all young, in their twenties, all were attractive, their hair was different. One was a blond, the other three were brunettes, but their hair wasn't quite the same color, one was very dark, almost black and the other two, including your friend, had brown hair."

"How were they dressed when their bodies were found?"

"All of them were dressed in the clothes they had been

wearing. The only thing I can think of is they were all stabbed. Do you have an idea about these murders?"

"Nothing the police don't already know," Paula said taking a sip of her coffee. "The killer is definitely a psychopath, who enjoys killing. His victims are victims of opportunity. There doesn't seem to any kind of pattern, but we would need to check on all of the victims' past to be sure. He sees this as some kind of game, and you are his path to glory."

"What does that mean?"

"It means you could be in danger. If we only had some clue to his identity."

"We do," Terry shouted. "The person you described, the one hanging around the receptionist's desk. He sounds like the person I saw at the fairgrounds where the second woman was murdered. The same place where your car got smashed."

"So?"

"What if it's the same guy?"

"You think the guy you saw at the fairgrounds is the same one who smashed my fender and is the killer? Why?"

"I don't know, I just do."

Paula leaned back in her chair. "I think you're grasping at straws. But still, I would like to find the jerk who smashed up my car. Of course, I would really like to find the guy who killed Kelly." Paula sipped of her coffee. "All right; let's do it. We'll look for this guy together. But I have to warn you; the guy who hit my car is probably not your killer."

"But we have nothing to lose, right?"

"Okay, we'll start tomorrow," Paula answered as she put the cap back on the bottle of whiskey and threw away the liquid left in her cup. "Right now, I want to go back and take care of Kelly. She deserves that."

Chapter Ten

The next morning Terry was reading the news clippings at Le Rue. Every few minutes he would look up to see if Paula had arrived. He had spent the rest of yesterday finishing up at the paper. He pulled everything he could from the files about the first three homicides. It seemed the victims had nothing in common. The first victim was Frances Colton, age 23, a clerk at Walmart. Emily Kemper was the second victim and the one Terry had seen in the flower dress. She was a 25-year old intern at a local hospital. She was engaged to a Navy doctor serving overseas. They had planned to be married when he returned from his current deployment. The third victim, Joyce Youngblood, was also 25 years old and working at a publishing house as an editor. The last victim was the receptionist, Kelly Richards, age 20, and a college student studying business administration. Because Terry had been there for the discovery of each body, he knew the women hadn't been sexually assaulted. Terry knew they were all killed with the same kind of knife. Terry kept looking for a connection between the victims, but the four women had nothing in common except for being stabbed to death by some deranged individual.

Terry's cell phone began to ring. Terry cautiously answered it.

"Terry, you need to get back here now."

"Who is this?" Terry asked.

"It's me, Steven Cornell. Your phone here rang, and it was the killer. He wanted to talk to you. When we told him you had taken the day off, he demanded we bring you into the office. He's going to call again in half an hour. So, get down here."

"I'll be there in a few minutes," Terry replied as he gathered his things and left the sidewalk café. Less than ten minutes later he walked into the editorial office.

"Glad you made it," Steven said. "He'll call back in a few minutes. Please try to keep him on the line as long as you can."

Terry nodded in agreement. He sat down at his desk, making sure he could easily reach his phone. He thought about turning on his computer and reading his email but decided against it. He didn't want anything to distract him. Even though reporters were working at their desks, Terry noticed they often looked up at him. It was only fifteen minutes, but it seemed like hours before the phone rang. Everyone stopped working when Terry picked up the phone.

"*City Times*, copyediting."

"Where have you been?" the voice demanded. "Why weren't you there when I called earlier?"

"I had the day off," Terry answered. "If I had known you were going to call, I would have made it a point to be here."

"Don't give me that," the voice yelled. "I don't like it when people play games with me."

"Hey, no one is playing any games."

"You had better not. Maybe I'll start calling another paper or news station. Then what will you do? Heh?"

"Look, no one here is playing games. It was just a case of me taking a day off. Come on, I have to take some time off. I had a dental appointment."

"All right, I'll let it go this time. Are the police still listening in?"

Terry glanced at Steven who signaled for him to give the killer an affirmative response. "Yeah, they're here. They're as interested as I am in hearing what you have to say."

"There's a book store on Fifth Avenue. It's called Fables. They specialize in used books. I hope you're a fan of Sherlock Holmes."

"Wait," Terry pleaded. "Where is this place? I've never heard of it."

"Time's up." The voice ended the call. Terry turned to Steven, who shook his head.

"Let's go," said Detective Marshall. "Let's see what we can find at that book store."

During the drive over, Marshall called into the dispatcher's office, who gave him the address of Fables Bookstore. It was a humble place with a large, wood-framed window displaying several old books around a manual typewriter. A small bell rang when Marshall opened the single wooden door to the shop. Along each wall were shelves filled with books. Down the center of the store were bookcases reaching to the ceiling. Hanging off each shelf was a single yellow cardboard sign stating the type of books on the shelf. Immediately to the left of the door, was a counter with an aged man sitting in a large stuffed chair, reading a book.

"Can I help you?" the man inquired.

Marshall showed the man his shield. "Do you have any Sherlock Holmes books?"

"Certainly," the aged individual replied. "Those are at the end of the center bookcase, on the right."

"Thanks," Marshall said as he and Terry started down the aisle. Marshall put on a pair of latex gloves and started going through the Sherlock Holmes novels. He pulled *The Memoirs of Sherlock Holmes* off the shelf. A single piece of paper fell to the ground. Marshall reached down and picked it up by the corner.

The rich spend too much money on frivolous things like

89

gym memberships to burn off the calories they gain from eating fancy food and expensive sweets. They spend money on spas and beauty parlors to pamper themselves and convince themselves they are beautiful when they are really pigs feeding off of the sweat and work of poor people. They think they are better than those who work for them because they can afford these wasteful things and real people have to do without.

The rich can hide behind their masks of wealth, but the common people are the ones with true beauty. Be sure to see them.

"This guy is nuts," Terry exclaimed.

"No, he's not," answered Marshall. "He's playing with us."

~ ~ ~

"They were victims of opportunity," Paula told Terry as they sat at Le Rue.

"How do you know?" Terry asked. "Did you talk to some kind of profiler?"

"It fits a pattern," Paula stated as she sat down. "The victims didn't have anything in common. They were just in the wrong place at the wrong time."

"Can you be sure? What about the clues he leaves in the books? It seems he has some kind of vendetta against rich people."

"Yes, I'm sure because Kelly, the receptionist at the gym, didn't have anything in common with the other victims. Also, Kelly wasn't wealthy. She was a college student, working her way through school. She shopped at Walmart, second-hand shops, and yard sales. Trust me; no one working at that gym is making much money. The bastard killed her just because she was there."

"So how are we going to catch him?"

"We're not," Paula replied leaning back in her chair.

"We're going to find the jerk that ran into my car. You seem to think he's your killer. I kind of hope so. It would be sweet justice to catch both the guy who wrecked my car and Kelly's killer."

"Yes, yes, but how are we going to do it?"

"First of all, don't you have to go to work?" Paula asked.

"No, I took some vacation time. The paper has someone else covering for me."

"Doesn't the guy call you whenever he kills someone? How are you going to answer the phone if you're with me?"

Terry held up his cell phone. "He called this morning when I was out of the office; so now I arranged for call forwarding. The police can't trace the call if I get it, but at least I will be able to answer the phone. Besides, he never stays on long enough for the police to trace the call. Hey, what about you? Don't you have to go to work?"

"No, because of Kelly's murder, the gym has closed down for a week. We want to give the police enough time to process the crime scene, then we'll have to clean up and stuff. Besides, right now, no one really wants to work. We're all kind of grieving."

Terry sat up and gathered the papers in front of him. "So, we can start now. Where do we go first?"

Paula pointed to Terry. "You go and get a phone book. We'll start with the Yellow Pages."

"Okay, I'll be right back. What are you going to do in the meantime?"

Paula chuckled. "I'm going to sit right here and finish my coffee."

~ ~ ~

Ashford kept sliding shirts on hangers along the sales rack. From this position, he was able to watch Terry and Paula sitting at the sidewalk café. Ashford smiled to himself when he saw Terry get up and walk away.

Ashford exited the shop and managed to cross the street

91

without attracting attention. He walked up to Paula. "Hey, fancy meeting you here?"

Paula set down the cup she was drinking from. "Morning. What can I do for you?"

"Nothing," Ashford answered. "I just noticed you here and thought I would say hello. By the way, I'm sorry to hear about your coworker."

"Thanks. Appreciate the sentiment."

"So, what are you doing?"

"Sorry?"

"What are you doing?"

"Sitting here drinking coffee," Paula replied with a bit of hostility in her voice.

"Hey, I'm just trying to be friendly."

"Sorry, but I'm a bit touchy since Kelly's death."

"Kelly?"

"My coworker, the one that was murdered."

Ashford raised his hands in mocked surrender. "Look, I obviously caught you at a bad time, so why don't we do this? How about tonight I take you out to dinner, give you a chance to relax, to unwind, to put this mess aside for a few hours?"

"Thanks, but no thanks."

"Come on. What have you got to lose? It's only dinner. Seriously, just a little bit of food, a little bit of wine, nothing more."

"Appreciate the offer, but I'm not really in the mood to go out."

Ashford leaned forward. "Hey, I understand. Your friend's death has got you down. But that is exactly the reason you should go out. You can't stay home and mope. It's unhealthy.

Paula took another sip of coffee. She looked at Ashford, silently for a moment. She took another sip of coffee and smiled. "Okay, tell you what. I'll meet you at the Fatten Ox.

How about seven thirty?"

"Sounds good. I'll see you then," Ashford said, waving goodbye to Paula.

~ ~ ~

"This is the sixth one," Terry complained. "All we have done is gone from one auto repair shop to another."

"It's called leg work," Paula replied. "Do you know how most crimes are solved?"

"Well, I've seen *CSI*, so I guess forensics gives the police most of their clues."

"Not even close. Most crimes get solved when someone gives the police a tip or some idea of who committed the crime. Other than that, they get solved through tenacious people following leads, checking out all the possibilities, and getting lucky."

"So, if you're stubborn, you solve crimes."

"Well, luck plays a big part in it. I remember I helped solve one burglary because I noticed what I thought was an abandoned car."

"Why did you think it was abandoned?"

"It didn't have any doors on it and it was covered with bondo," Paula replied. "I thought it had broken down."

"So, when the burglars came out, you arrested them?"

"No, I placed a ticket on it. If it wasn't moved in three days, then I would have had it towed. It turns out that was the car the burglars were using. When the burglary was reported the next day, I heard about it and told the detective handling the case about the car. They put out a BOLO for it, and it wasn't hard to find. When a patrol officer pulled over, they found stolen property in the back seat."

"What's a BOLO?"

"*Be on the lookout*. They used to call it an *all-points bulletin*."

"So, the case was solved because you were lucky."

"That's right," Paula stated. "Another case I worked on

was an armed robbery. The only clue we had the suspect drove off in a white car with a Marine Corps sticker on the back bumper. I went to the recruiters and got one of every sticker they had. Went back to our witness who showed me which sticker it was. Then I drove all over the base looking at every white car to see if it had that sticker on it rear bumper."

"Did you find it?"

"Yep, found three of them. Fortunately, the witness said it was on the passenger side of the car and that limited it down to one. We got a picture of the driver when he came through the gate and the witness identified him in a photo lineup."

"Okay," said Terry. "Your point is?"

"My point is that police work is not like it is on television. Most cases are solved either through luck or tenacity. They don't always find clues listed in a data base. They aren't able to lift fingerprints, and even if they do, often there are so many, they wouldn't be able to identify any single individual. Even if they did, all fingerprints prove is the person was there; so, if that person has a reason to be there, then the fingerprints prove nothing."

"So, autopsy reports, forensics, crime scene investigations and all that stuff is useless?"

"No," Paula stated adamantly, "all of that helps lead to conviction once someone is arrested."

"But it doesn't help with the case."

"No, it does help. There are clues found at crime scenes, and sometimes they do give police officers leads to who might be a suspect. But, and this is the important part, real life isn't like it is on TV. While autopsy reports and forensics help, it still takes hard work, skill, luck, and perseverance to solve cases. Let's take a look at the clues our killer has left us. So far, the only one we have is he might be the guy in the blue pickup truck that might have smashed into my car. So, we are going to all of the auto body shops hoping to find a part from a blue pickup. So, quit complaining and let's check this place out."

Terry reluctantly got out of Paula's car. He stood by the car as Paula pushed the key lock and walked around to the back of the body shop. The owner of the shop stepped out into the parking lot, watched Paula go around back, before looking at Terry.

"Where is she going?" the owner asked. "We don't have any public restrooms."

"No, nothing like that. She just wants to see what stuff you have in the back of the shop."

The owner glared at Terry, wipes his hands on a rag he was holding, and started to go after Paula. He got to the corner of the shop when Paula returned.

"What were you doing back there?" the owner demanded.

"Just checking on something."

"Checking on what?" the owner barked.

Paula took four steps pass the man before turning to face him. She took a deep breath and smiled. "Several days ago, a blue pickup truck smashed into my car. When I got it fixed, I realized many times body shops swap out one damaged part for another from a different vehicle, the same make and year model and the original. I was looking to see if you had anything from a blue pickup in the back."

"You could have asked." The owner said with hostility in his voice.

"Sorry, I didn't think it was an issue," Paula replied. "But since we're here, could you tell us if you have done any work on a blue pickup?"

"Why do you care?"

"Like I said, it was a blue pickup that hit my car."

"Not that it's any of your business, but no," the owner answered.

"In that case, thank you for your time," Paula said as she opened the door to her car. Terry didn't wait; he immediately got in.

"Boy that guy was certainly unfriendly," Terry said as they left the body shop.

"Yeah he was. It goes with the territory. Some people are protective of their turf." Paula pointed to the phone book in Terry's lap. "What the next one?"

Terry told her as she drove down the street.

~ ~ ~

"Yeah, what do you want?" the voice said.

"Is that the way you answer your phone?"

"Who are you and what do you want?"

"This is Tom O'Donnell, the guy who fixed your truck."

"How did you get this number?"

"You left your registration in your truck. Yeah, that's right, I know your real name, address, everything."

"I paid you, so what's the problem?"

"Look I know you didn't want to report your *accident* to the insurance company."

"So?"

"Well, there were two people here asking about a blue pickup, a blue pickup with body damage from an accident."

"Who were they? Were they cops?"

"Nah. One of them was a tall blond woman. The other one was really short. The blond looked around and asked some questions. What's going on? Why are there people looking for you?"

"Relax will you. Look I smashed into another car and it's probably the owner looking to see if she can find me and get me to pay for the damages. You didn't tell them anything, did you?"

"No. I figured whatever went down is between you and the woman whose car you hit. But I thought I should let you know what happened."

"Was the woman good looking?"

"Man, you are really warped."

"Was she good looking?"

"Not really. She wasn't ugly, but she was so tall."

"What about the guy?"

"He was really short. Like a midget."

"Really, I think I know who you're talking about. What kind of car were they driving?"

"A 2016 silver Ford Fiesta. There isn't going to be any trouble, is there?"

"Not for you."

"There better not be."

"What do you mean?"

"You came in here, gave a false name and address, paid in cash, and insisted I keep this between the two of us. Now someone comes around and asks questions. It had better not be anything more than a person trying to settle an insurance claim. I don't mind helping a fellow out, but not if it's going to come back to bite me. So, is there anything more I should know about your accident?"

"You mean did I hit somebody and flee the scene of an accident? No. I smashed someone's fender and just didn't want to deal with insurance companies. That's it."

"Okay, as long as it doesn't cause me any problems, then we're cool."

"Thanks," said the voice as he hung up his phone. The voice stared at his phone for a minute thinking about the conversation. He realized he would have to do something about this situation.

Chapter Eleven

Damn *it* thought Paula pounding her head against a pillow. *What was going through my mind?* She looked over at the sleeping body next to her.

The night had started off pleasant enough. She met Ashford at the Fatten Ox, a trending English pub known for having Guinness on tap and great food. Paula enjoyed Glenkinchie, a 12-year-old scotch. Ashford tried to impress her by ordering Cardhu, an 18-year-old single malt.

Strangely enough Paula enjoyed the evening. Maybe she drank too much. Maybe Ashford was really charming. No Paula realized. Kelly's death had haunted her throughout the evening. She needed to do something, anything, to feel alive. Sleeping with Ashford seemed like a good idea last night, but in the morning light, Paula realized the foolishness of the idea. Her damn VA therapist was going to have a field day over this.

Paula threw off the covers. She put on some sweat pants and a tee shirt before going to the kitchen and turning on the coffee maker. Paula groaned and leaned against the kitchen sink.

"Hey honey."

Paula looked over at Ashford, standing there naked with his arms outstretched. "If you're waiting for coffee, it's going to be a few minutes, so you can put your clothes back on."

"Hey, baby. There's no need for the fun to end. Wasn't it good last night?"

Paula smiled, walked over to Ashford, and kissed him. "It was great honey. But I have things to do, and don't you have to go to work?"

"Don't worry," Ashford said waving his hand. "I can go in late. No one is going to care."

Paula patted Ashford's chest. "Get dressed. The coffee will be ready in a minute."

Ashford returned to the bedroom.

"I don't have anything for breakfast, but if you want, we can grab something at a diner nearby," Paula said as she poured coffee into two cups.

"Are you trying to get rid of me?" Ashford yelled from the bedroom.

Paula took a sip of coffee, closed her eyes, and sighed deeply. "I'm not trying to get rid of you. I have things to do. Come on. Last night was great, but today is a whole new day."

"Can I see you again?" Ashford asked as he entered the kitchen. "Maybe tonight or this weekend?"

"Not tonight, but maybe another time. We'll see."

Ashford quickly kissed Paula and grabbed a cup of coffee. "Well, if you're busy, then I guess I should go to work. Still got news to write about."

"That's right," Paula said gently guiding Ashford to the door. "The news waits for no man, or something like that. Take care and have a good day."

Ashford opened the door, turned and gave Paula another quick kiss. "Try not to miss me too much."

"I'll try," Paula replied as she shut the door after Ashford. "Actually, I don't think that's going to be a problem," she said to herself.

~ ~ ~

Terry called her Mrs. Dalmatian because of whenever he saw her, she was walking her Dalmatian. The dog was very friendly and always came up to Terry for attention and affection. This morning Terry was walking back and forth in front of his apartment building. He smiled and waved at Mrs. Dalmatian but didn't pet the dog. As they walked away, the dog seemed depressed at being ignored. Terry continued to pace back and forth.

Paula pulled up to the curb and Terry jumped into the car. "You're late," Terry said as he buckled his seatbelt.

"Had a rough night."

"Why? What did you do?"

"Never mind. It's really none of your business."

Terry sighed. "All right. Let's go."

"You need to switch to decafe," Paula replied. "We have all day to cover the rest of the body shops. By the way, how many are left?"

"Seven. But we might also want to check out junkyards and there is an auto body shop at the high school. They train kids to work on cars and stuff."

"Not a bad idea," Paula replied as she pulled away from the curb. Terry busied himself with the phone book and finding the address of the first body shop they would visit. When Terry looked up to tell Paula the address, he realized she knew where to go.

They passed a junkyard, and Terry made a mental note they should return to it later. They came to a stop sign. Paula out of habit looked in her rearview mirror and saw a pickup approaching. She started through the intersection. The pickup rammed the back of Paula's car, backed off, and rammed it again.

Terry turned in panic. "It's a blue pickup! It's the killer!"

Paula silently cursed herself. She should have realized the danger when she first saw the pickup. She knew it was blue, but it failed to register with her that it might be the one they were looking for. Right now, her focus was on keeping the car on the road.

The truck speed up and pulled alongside Paula. She

glanced at the driver. He was wearing a hooded Halloween mask. While she couldn't see his face, she was sure he was grinning as he swerved over and smashed into the driver's side of the car. Paula turned the steering wheel to counter the push of the truck. The truck separated from Paula's car for about three feet and turned again to smash into Paula. This time it forced the car off the road into a small ditch. The pickup squealed to a stop about forty feet away.

Paula focused on catching her breath. She unbuckled her seatbelt and reached into the glove department. Terry stared in amazement when she pulled out an automatic pistol. Paula flung open her door, rolled out of the car onto the ground and leveled the weapon at the man in the Halloween mask as he got out of his pickup. Paul fired without taking aim. She missed the man, but still managed to hit the tailgate of the truck. The driver turned and jumped back into the pickup and drove off. Paula slowly stood up with the weapon at her side. She turned to see Terry was still buckled into the passenger's seat.

"You okay?" she asked.

Terry pointed to the truck that had disappeared. "He tried to kill us."

Paula gave Terry one of those tell-me-something-I don't-know look.

"He tried to kill us," Terry yelled. "What are we going to do?"

Paula walked around her car, inspecting the damage. Her back end was smashed, but the trunk remained closed. While the driver's side of the car had several scrapes and dents, the doors still opened and closed.

Terry, still belted in the passenger seat, watched Paula as she circled her car. He unbuckled his seatbelt and jumped out of the car. "Well, what are we going to do? What if he comes back?"

Paula held up her pistol. "We should be so lucky. He's

not coming back, not after I took a shot at him. He wasn't prepared for that. In the meantime, I'll call a tow truck and get them to pull us out of this ditch."

"Then we'll call the police," Terry demanded.

"Yeah, yeah, we'll call the police."

~ ~ ~

It took an hour before the tow truck arrived. It took them less than ten minutes to get Paula's car out of the ditch. They were kind enough to wait around and followed Paula for about a mile to ensure her car was fit to drive. By that time, Paula and Terry were only a few minutes from the police station. Upon arrival, Paula asked the desk sergeant if they could talk to a detective. The desk sergeant asked them to wait. Twenty minutes later, Terry and Paula were still waiting.

Paula was leaned against the back of the bench with her legs stretched out in front of her. She appeared to be napping. Terry was on the bench next to her, with his feet crossed and swinging his legs back and forth, waiting for one of the detectives to come and get them.

"Stop that," Paula complained. "I'm trying to sleep."

"How can you sleep?" Terry asked with irritation. "We were almost killed. We need to get the police out there looking for the killer."

Paula opened one eye and turned her head slightly to look at Terry. She then closed her eye and resumed her original position.

Detective Marshall came out before Terry worked up enough courage to hit Paula in the arm to wake her. "Sorry to keep you waiting. I was told you wanted to speak to me."

"Yes," said Terry jumping off the bench. "We were run off the road by the killer. We are getting close to solving the case."

Paula sat up, yawned, and stretched out her arms. "He's right, almost. A couple of hours ago a blue pickup truck ran us off the road. I wouldn't be surprised if it was the same truck that smashed in my fender at the fairgrounds."

"You sure about this?" Marshall asked.

"Take a look at my car. The attack was deliberate."

"Did you get a look at the driver?"

"Yes and no," Paula answered. "I saw the driver, but he was wearing a hooded Halloween mask. He wanted to make sure I couldn't identify him. Also, I tried to get a look at his license plate. It was covered up."

"Anything distinctive about the truck?"

"It's a blue pickup, no more than three or four years old, and it has a bullet hole in the tailgate. I'm sure there's damage to the passenger side of the truck. He slammed into my car with the truck, so you might want to take some paint samples."

Marshall looked up at the ceiling and took a deep breath. "How did it get a bullet hole in its tailgate?"

Paula pulled out her wallet and showed Marshall a license to carry permit. "My weapon is in my car if you want to run any ballistics."

"And what makes you think this guy who ran you off the road is also the killer we're looking for?"

Paula smiled at Marshall. "We were checking body shops to see if we could find the guy who smashed my car. We must have come close to identifying him. No one is going to kill us because of a smashed fender, especially when we don't know who he is. So, it has to be something more important than an insurance claim, such as a murder. Somehow we spooked him."

"If it was the killer, perhaps we should get Mr. Lambert back to the paper in case he calls."

"Yes," said Terry.

"Don't bother," replied Paula. "The driver saw me and Terry in the car. He won't call today. Probably tomorrow, but not today."

Marshall nodded in agreement. "You know, you would make a pretty good detective."

"If that's a job offer, I'm not interested," Paula said as she stood up. "If there isn't anything else, I think we should be going."

"Just one more question. How did the driver know where to find you?"

"Don't really know," Paula answered. "I'm guessing he knew most of the auto body shops are along Carlton Street. He could have waited there until I came by and then followed me. If you know what kind of car I drive, I'm fairly easy to spot."

"I guess it's possible." Marshall watched them as they left. He went back to his desk and typed in a background request for Paula Stanford.

~ ~ ~

Paula and Terry sat in her car in the police parking lot. Terry watched as Paula closed her eyes and leaned back against the headrest. A crime scene technician was taking some paint samples from the Paula's car. After a few minutes, he signaled he was finished, and they could leave. Paula nodded to him and leaned her head back against the headrest.

Terry tried to be patient. "What are you thinking," he asked.

"That I just got this car fixed and now I have to do it again. Someone up there doesn't like me."

"That's what's bothering you? Do you have any idea what it means that we were attacked?"

Paula turned her head to face Terry. "We ran into somebody yesterday who knew the person who smashed my car. And it seems you're right, the guy who smashed my car is also the killer. Now, how do we find out who we talked to yesterday talked to the killer? We could go back, but I doubt anyone would tell us more today than they did yesterday."

"I have an idea," Terry replied. "Providing you don't mind lending your car to someone."

"Talk to me."

"I could call Diana; she's a reporter I work with."

"Yeah, I know her."

"We give her your car, and she goes around to the same body shops that we did yesterday. She gives them the same story you did. A blue pickup truck ran into her car. It's obvious from the damage. She asks for estimates for the repairs. When she leaves, we wait to see if the shop owner contacts the owner of the pickup truck."

"Great idea except for the fact that the owner could be calling anyone. We would never know if it's the killer or his wife."

"Could we plant a bug?"

"Not on every shop we visited. Still, now that I think about it, maybe your idea will work."

~ ~ ~

Diana pulled into a shopping center parking lot. She found Paula and Terry sitting in Paula's car.

"My goodness, what happened?" Diana asked as she got out of her car.

"Got ran off the road," Paula answered. "That's why we need your help. Yesterday, Terry and I went to several body shops looking for the blue pickup that smashed my fender the night the woman was killed at the fairgrounds. This morning, a blue pickup ran me off the road. If you're willing to help us, I'd like for you to go to the same body shops we went to yesterday. You drive my car; I'll drive yours. After you visit each shop, we'll watch to see what the people do. Hopefully, we'll be able to tell which one calls the owner of the blue pickup truck."

"How will you know if he is calling the owner of the truck or someone else? I mean he could be ordering a pizza for all you know."

"Timing," Paula explained. "If you hit the body shop where the truck was repaired, the owner will call the killer as soon as you leave. Also, your body language is going to be a lot different from when you are calling your wife or ordering a pizza."

"That's true," Diana agreed. "Where do we start?"

Paula gave Diana her keys and a piece of paper with addresses on it. "Let's start with this one. He seemed angry at us for asking questions yesterday. I thought it was just a case of the person being territorial, but now I think it might be something else. You go and ask about a blue pickup. Tell him it smashed into you and you're looking for it. If he gives any information, great. If not, just leave and we'll meet you down the block."

Diana smiled as she handed Paula the keys to her car. "Sounds like a plan."

Diana drove to the body shop. Paula and Terry parked in a shopping center parking lot across the street.

The body shop owner approached Diana as she got out of the car. He took notice of her pale blue skirt and white blouse, which highlighted her figure and her good looks. It was a sharp contrast to the silver Ford with the driver's side bashed in. "Good grief. What happened to your car?"

"You won't believe it," Diana said waving her hand towards the damage. "This morning, a blue pickup truck ran me off the road. That driver was crazy. He didn't even stop. Fortunately, the car still runs, but the damage is quite extensive. Can you give me an estimate on the repairs?"

"Will it be covered by insurance?"

"I hope so," Diana answered. "But if a blue pickup comes in, could you please call me? If I can find him, then I can get his insurance to pay for this. I already filed a police report."

The body shop owner went into his office and returned with a clipboard. He walked around the car, making notes as he inspected the damage. He returned to his office, looked through a few catalogs before bringing an estimate to Diana.

She thanked him and drove off. The owner watched Diana drive out of sight, then went back to his office.

~ ~ ~

"Who is this?"

"You really need to work on your telephone manners," the body shop owner said. "This is O'Donnell, the guy who worked on your car. The same one who called you yesterday about the two people looking for you and your truck."

"Yeah, I remember."

"Someone else came in today, also looking for someone driving a blue pickup. I saw the paint and it matches the color of your truck."

"So?"

"This lady said you tried to run her off the road."

The voice could tell the person on the other end of the phone was angry. "Was it the same person as yesterday?"

"No, it was someone else. What are you doing?"

"It's none of your business. What kind of car was she driving?"

"Hey, I'm doing you a solid," the body shop owner yelled.

"Okay. But what kind of car?"

"A 2016 silver Ford Fiesta, license number WMD 849. Did you run her off the road this morning?"

"That's the same car you called me about yesterday."

"Yeah, I know. That's why I'm calling you again, today."

"Can you describe the driver?"

"Yeah, she was in her late 20's, fairly good looking, brunette, average height. Why?"

"No reason."

"You still haven't answered my question. Did you run her off the road this morning?"

The voice hung up. He slowly walked to the window in his living room and looked out onto the street. The car was the same, but the driver was not. Something was going on, and he didn't like it.

Chapter Twelve

Paula watched the shop owner through a pair of binoculars. Terry was kneeling on the passenger seat, leaning forward, hands on the dashboard, trying to get a better view.

"Will you sit down?" Paula demanded. "You're distracting me. What's worse, you're bringing attention to us by standing on the seat."

"I want to see."

Paula handed the binoculars to Terry.

"He's on the phone."

"I can see that," Paula said.

"He seems angry." Terry said as the body shop owner slammed down the phone.

"Give me back the binoculars," Paula demanded. Terry handed them to her. Paula stared through them for a few minutes. "Call Diana We've got to meet up. And then, depending on how adventurous you are, I have an idea.

~ ~ ~

Murphy's was crowded, as usual. Terry and Paula were grateful to arrive and discover Diana had a table for them. A perky young blond waitress came over and took their orders.

"Do you have any idea on who smashed into your car?" Diana asked after the waitress left.

"Not yet," Paula answered. "But at the first shop you went to, the guy acted like he knew the driver. When you left, the owner made a phone call, and from his body language, he seemed upset."

"So how do we get him to tell us who was driving the blue truck?" Terry whispered, leaning forward on the table.

The perky waitress returned with their drinks. Paula waited until the waitress left before answering. "I have an idea, but it involves some risks. I'm willing to take them, but what about you? And I am serious about there being some risks."

"Hey, that sound's interesting," a voice replied. Terry let out a heavy sigh. The last thing he wanted was for Ashford to show up. "Hey, babe. How's it going?" Ashford said greeting everyone.

"Hey yourself," Paula answered.

Terry and Diana looked at Paula. "Is there something we should know?" Terry asked.

"Hey Runt, mind your own business," Ashford responded as he sat down.

"Please don't ask," Paula replied. "It's embarrassing, and it has nothing to do with the case."

Diana took a gulp of her drink. "Well, let's move onto another topic of conversation. Paula, you said had an idea of how to find the guy in the pickup truck. You mentioned something about risks."

"Who's this guy in a pickup?" Ashford asked.

"None of your business," Terry answered.

Paula held up her hand to cut off Ashford before he could respond. "Terry thinks the guy who smashed into my car is the same one who is killing all of the young ladies, especially since a guy in blue pickup ran us off the road this morning."

"Wait a minute," Ashford interjected. "The guy who has been calling the paper, killing the girls, is the same one who ran into you. And you know what kind of pickup he drives. Why haven't the police made an arrest yet?"

"We've told the police everything, and they're working on it. But no one knows who he is yet."

Ashford smiled. "You have a plan on how to find him? What is it?"

"The fewer who know, the better, and safer, it is for everyone," was Paula response.

~ ~ ~

As a combat Marine serving in Iraq, Paula had taken risks. She had also placed others in dangerous situations. But this one was plain foolish.

Terry, Paula, and Diana spent the day visiting various body shops, just to be through. Fifteen minutes before closing, Diana returned to the suspected body shop with Terry hiding in the back seat. Diana met the owner in the parking lot and asked to check the office to see if she left her phone there. Terry could tell the owner was suspicious as he watched as the owner shook his head, informing Diana there was no phone in the office. Diana smiled and moved passed the owner, insisting on checking herself. The owner followed. Terry snuck out of the car and ran into the garage. He desperately looked around and found a place to hide behind two stacks of tires. He hoped the smell of new rubber and grease wouldn't make him sneeze and reveal his position. Diana left, the owner closed the shop, finished the day's paperwork, and left. Then came the hard part, waiting until dark.

Paula and Diana pulled into the body shop parking lot an hour after sunset. There was a single street lamp illuminating the parking lot along with two lights shining on the body shop's name above the door and the garage. Diana called Terry on her cell phone. He came through the shop to unlock the door, letting Paula and Diana in. A quick look around convinced Paula their entrance had been unobserved and there were no alarm systems. Diana started going through the one file cabinet in the office while Terry kept a look out. Paula searched the desk for any phone numbers she could find. She copied all of them down in a notebook.

"Found something," Diana whispered.

"You don't need to whisper," Paula stated. "There's no one here except us."

"I can't help it," she continued to whisper. "I'm committing a crime and I don't feel comfortable shouting about it."

"Never mind," Terry responded in a strong whisper. "What did you find?"

"I found a bill for a pickup truck, dated a week ago. There is a name and an address."

"Anything else?" Paula asked.

"Nah, I went back two weeks, before the murder at the fairgrounds. I figured anything before then wasn't connected to the case. This is the only thing I found."

"Great," Paula said, "give it here so I can copy down the name and address."

"Don't we want to take this with us?" Terry asked still whispering.

"Why?" Paula asked. "All we need is a name and address. Anything else is useless."

"It proves he got his truck fixed here," Diana stressed.

"Yes, it does, but if we take it, the police will never find it," Paula explained. "Without that piece of paper, they can't get a warrant. Without a warrant, they can't search the person's house and make an arrest. If this guy is our killer, then we have to make sure he gets caught, *and convicted.*"

Paula handed the receipt back to Diana who replaced in the files. Paula took one quick look around to make sure they didn't leave anything behind. She signaled for them all to leave.

~ ~ ~

The two patrol officers couldn't believe their luck. A call had come in reporting a burglary at an auto repair shop. The burglars were still there when they arrived. This was certainly an odd group of burglars, a tall blond, a dwarf, and an attractive woman wearing a skirt. Their getaway car was easy to recognize with all of the damage done to the driver's side and the broken taillights. The officers smiled. They had a traffic violation and more than enough reason to stop the vehicle and its occupants. The patrol car remained in the shadows and watched the suspects get in their car and pull out onto the street. The patrol car followed for two blocks before turning on their flashing lights.

~ ~ ~

Ashford grinned when the police arrived in response to his anonymous phone call. From his vantage point, he could see both the patrol car and Terry, Paula, and Diana in the office. He watched as they left the body shop and patrol car began following them. He was delighted when the police officers pulled Paula and her colleagues over.

~ ~ ~

Paula cursed herself as soon as she saw the patrol cruiser pull in behind her. When they turned on their flashing lights, she pulled over to the curb and turned off the engine.

"We're in trouble, aren't we," Terry stated.

"Depends on your point of view," Paula responded. "If being under arrest is an issue, then we're in trouble."

One of the patrol officers approached the driver's door. He stopped behind the driver's door, forcing Paula to look over her left shoulder. The second officer stopped about three feet from the right rear fender, giving him a clear view of the other two occupants in the car.

"Can I see your license and registration?" the first officer asked. Paula knew it was not a request. She pulled the registration from the visor above her and took her license out of her wallet.

The officer took them and quickly examined them. "You want to tell me what you were doing at that body shop back there?"

"No," Paula stated.

"Step out of the vehicle please."

Paula pulled the keys out of the ignition and placed them on the dashboard. She slowly opened her door and stepped out to follow the officer to the back of her vehicle. A second patrol unit arrived at the scene.

"I observed you and your passengers inside the body shop," the first officer said. "I know you don't work there. Now you have the right to remain silent, but if there is a reasonable explanation, I would love to hear it."

Paula turned around and placed her hands behind her back. "There isn't," she answered over her shoulder. "Just take it easy; we won't resist."

Two other officers took Diana and Terry out of the vehicle and placed them in cuffs.

"Don't say anything," Paula said to them. "Just cooperate and we'll work this out at the station." She turned to the officer. "I need to tell you I have a nine-millimeter automatic in the glove department. I have a license for it in my wallet. Also, the keys to the car are on the dashboard. I would appreciate it if one of you could park it in the shopping center parking lot over there. I'd like to save myself the towing charges."

"You seem to know exactly what to do," the officer said. "Guess this isn't your first rodeo."

"I watch a lot of cop shows," Paula replied.

Chapter Thirteen

"Thanks," Detective Marshall angrily said as he entered the room where Paula, Diana, and Terry were sitting. "It's not like I need any sleep. So of course, getting phone calls from the desk sergeant in the middle of the night is something I look forward to."

"Sorry about that," Terry said meekly.

"Sorry! Sorry doesn't cut it. What the hell were you doing?!" Marshall yelled.

"We were following a lead," Diana started to explain.

"Who are you?" interrupt Marshal still yelling at the three of them.

"I'm Diana Hawley. I'm a reporter for the *City Times*. We've met when you've been there. Don't you remember?"

"Who cares," Marshal said with animosity. "I have three people, no idiots, who broke into a body shop, which is a felony by the way, got caught by a patrol unit, and have absolutely no reason for being there. But you're lucky. For some odd reason the owner doesn't want to press charges. He thinks you've learned your lesson. Well I don't. I should lock you all up for the night just to teach you a lesson."

"But we were following a lead, and I think we found the serial killer you and Terry are looking for," Diana countered.

"No you haven't," Marshall stated leaning forward till his face was a few inches from Diana's. "Whatever you found, we can't use it. It will get thrown out in court. Even if we catch the guy, he will go free because the evidence you found was illegally obtained."

"And you know better," Marshall continued, this time focusing his wrath at Paula. Marshall picked up a folder from the table in front of him. "Sergeant Paula Stanford, United States Marine Corps, honorably discharged, served as a military police officer for six years, awarded the Silver Star and the Purple Heart. You even worked CID and completed an associate's degree in criminal justice."

Marshall then turned to face Terry. "And you! What are you? You're an editor at a newspaper. If it weren't for your connection to this case, I would ... I would..." Marshall threw his hands up in the air. "What am I going to do with you?"

"Listen to us," Diana immediately answered. "We know who the killer is."

Marshall sat down across the table from the three. "Okay, tell me what you've got."

"Let me," Paula said holding up her hand to signal Diana and Terry to be quiet. "The night of the murder at the fairgrounds, someone smashed in the fender of my car. I almost got run over by a blue pickup, which we thought might have been the car that hit mine. Terry and I thought maybe if we could find the body shop that repaired the damage to the truck, we might get a lead on the killer; certainly, a lead on the person who smashed my car. Yesterday, a blue pickup truck deliberately ran us off the road. We figured we had found the body shop where the pickup was repaired."

"Old news. You told me all of that when you were here reporting the incident.

"That's right," Paula continued. "So, we went back and snuck in to see if we could find anything in the records at the shop. We didn't take anything. We didn't cause any damage. All we did was look through the guy's files. That's it. We did find a name and an address for a repair to a blue pickup. Of course, we got arrested right afterwards, so we haven't checked it out yet."

"Yes, don't you see," Diana added. "That's why the owner doesn't want to press charges. He's afraid if you investigate, you'll find the identity of the killer, who is trying to hide. It's obvious the body shop owner is an accomplice or blackmailing the killer."

Marshall silently continued to stare at the three of them.

"We found the killer," Terry shout throwing his hands out in front of him.

Marshall looked at his watch, then stood up. "I'll have one of the patrol officers to come in and take your statements."

"Then we can go?" Terry asked.

"Oh no," Marshall answered. "You're going to give your statements, then you are going to wait until I return. The last thing I want is for you three to be running around causing any more trouble."

"You mean we have to spend the night here?" Diana said with surprise.

Marshal leaned over the table. "You committed a felony. You're getting a break by no one pressing charges. So yes, I am keeping you here, and out of trouble, so that I can get some sleep before I have to come back in the morning."

~ ~ ~

"Whoever this is, it had better be important. It's the middle of the night."

"It's Tom O'Donnell, the guy who fixed your truck."

"Why are you calling me?"

"You really need to work on your social skills," Tom replied. "I'm calling because that favor I did for you is coming back to bite me in the ass."

"What do you mean?"

"I just got finished with the police. It turns out those people who were asking about you a couple of days ago broke into my shop. The police caught them. I had the police all over my shop, but it doesn't seem anything is missing. Still, the police were here, and there is a chance they may come back."

"What were they looking for in your shop?"

"I'm guessing they were looking for some kind of evidence that I fixed your truck."

"They didn't find anything, did they? You didn't keep any kind of record, did you?"

"Just a bill, under the false name and address you gave me."

"What! Why did you do that? There wasn't supposed to be any kind of record."

"Hey, when you came in here, you told me it was just a simple case of not wanting to report it to your insurance company. So yes, I did keep a record. This is a business that requires me to pay taxes. But don't worry. Like I said, the bill and everything is under that false name you gave me. Now, I'm wondering if this favor I did for you is going to come back and land me in jail. This shop is all I have. I can't afford to lose it."

"Don't worry. It's an insurance case like I said, nothing more. The police aren't going to get involved."

"You sure?"

"Yes, I'm sure." The man hung up. He didn't like the auto shop calling him, especially in the middle of the night and with news about people trying to find out who he is. He got dressed. He knew he had to handle the situation.

~ ~ ~

"Sign here," the desk sergeant said pointing to the bottom of the form. "It's a receipt for your property."

"Thanks," Paula said signing the form. Terry and Diana already had their belongings.

The desk sergeant took the form from Paula and put it with the rest of the paperwork. "Okay. That's it. You're free to go."

Diana led the trio out of the police station. "I'll get us a taxi," she said as she pulled out her cell phone and punched in some numbers.

"While we're waiting, mind if I ask you a question," Terry asked Paula.

"Yes, but you're going to anyway, so go ahead," Paula replied with some frustration.

Terry took a deep breath. "You were a military police officer. You know a lot about investigations. But you work as a fitness instructor. Why don't work for a police department?"

Paula stared at Terry. For a long minute she didn't say anything. "I really don't want to discuss it."

"Seriously, why aren't you?" Terry continued to inquire. "You would make a great cop."

Diana finished her call. "Terry's got a point. Why aren't you a cop?"

"It's personal," Paula answered.

"We just spent the night together," Terry joked. "We got arrested together. It's a fair question."

Paula looked around, taking a moment to collect her thoughts.

"Something happened," Diana added. "What happened?"

"I got wounded in Iraq. After that I became bitter, really angry. Here we were trying to help people and it seemed the more we tried, the more we got shot at. I saw the world divided into two parts: us the good guys, them the bad guys. But it wasn't just Iraq. Remember, as a cop, I dealt with criminals, people you would never want to take home to meet your family. Then there are the victims. Some of them are naïve, others expect you to solve problems they are responsible for. You spend your time drinking with other cops, bitching about the work, growing more disillusioned with society every day."

"But you seemed to understand what was happening," Terry interjected. "You could have done something about it."

"It's not that simple," Paula replied. "There was a burglary. Someone stole more than a hundred thousand dollars-worth of equipment. I was sure it this one Marine. He was a drug user, had access to the stuff, and wasn't really one of your better Marines. For more than a week, I harassed him, brought him in every chance I could get, trying to get him to break and confess. Then we found him, dead, from a drug overdose. Whether it was accidental or suicide, no one really knows. Two days later, we got a break in the case. The guy I was after, he was completely innocent. The worst part was I didn't care. *A person died, and I didn't care.* I'm not sure which I hate most, the bad guys or me. I can't go back to being a cop. It made me hate the world. Now I'm trying to become a normal human being, at least someone who doesn't hate humanity."

"You don't seem that angry," Terry replied.

"Trust me," Paula answered. "I can't remember the last time I wasn't miserable. And this case with a banged-up car and Kelly's murder isn't helping."

~ ~ ~

"Here come the jailbirds," Ashford said laughing as Terry and Diana walked into the editorial office.

"Stuff it," Diana said throwing her purse on her desk and flopping down in her chair.

Ashford took a sip of coffee. "What about you, Runt? You got something to say?"

Terry leaned back in his chair. "Yeah, at the police station, I met the scrum of the earth, dregs of society. They seemed to know you."

"Hey Runt!"

"Stop calling me that!"

"Both of you, behave yourselves," Diana demanded. "Let's just get to work."

Fitch came out of his office. "Hey Ashford, got a story for you. There's a fire over on Carlton Street. Get over there, get some photos and the story."

Ashford set his coffee down and grabbed a camera along with a notebook before running out the door. Diana and Terry exchanged looks. "Wasn't that shop we were at on Carlton Street?" Diana asked.

"Yeah, it was."

Diana grabbed her purse. Fitch watched as Terry and Diana headed to the door. "Where are you two going?" he demanded.

"We're chasing a story," Diana yelled as they ran out the door.

~ ~ ~

"Well, I've got two of the Three Musketeers, where's the third one?"

Diana and Terry turned to see Marshall standing behind them. "Well, where is she?"

"Don't know," Terry answered.

"What are you two doing here?" Ashford demanded as he approached the group. "I'm covering the story."

Diana put her hand up. "Relax, we're not here to steal your story."

"Why are you here?" Ashford continued to demand.

Marshall stepped in front of Ashford. "They're here to talk to me. Now you need to go back and join the rest of the reporters. As soon as we have a statement, you will be informed."

"You can't control me. *Freedom of the Press*." Ashford stated smugly.

"*Interfering with a police investigation*," Marshall replied, taking out his handcuffs. Marshall watched as

121

Ashford reluctantly returned to the other reporters. Marshall turned his attention to Terry and Diana. "He had a good point. What are you doing here?"

"This is the shop where the killer got his truck fixed," Terry answered. "The killer's name and address are in the records in there."

Marshall pointed to the smoldering building. "I know this is the shop you broke into last night. No, the records may have been there. Now they are nothing more than ash. The fire completely destroyed everything."

"The owner must have burned it down to destroy the evidence," Terry exclaimed. As soon as he said it, he realized the foolishness of the statement. Why burn down the entire building if you needed to destroy a few sheets of paper?

"Why are the police here?" Diana asked. "I understand the need for traffic control, but why are you here?"

"Call it a hunch," Marshall replied. "You burglarize the place. The owner refuses to press charges. Now there's a fire at the same location. There is no way this is a coincidence."

Diana watched the fire department as they were finishing up and repacking their equipment on their trucks. "Where's the owner? Shouldn't he be here? If it were my business, I would be here, even if it was being burned down."

"We haven't been able to locate him yet," Marshall said. "But I've got a feeling, we're going to find him soon."

"You mean you think he's in the fire; that's horrible," Diana shouted.

"All right," said Marshall. "Let's think about this. There is no reason for a fire if the owner simply wanted to get rid of some evidence. He could shred it or burn it in a barbecue grill. I doubt the owner would decide to commit arson and insurance fraud, especially when the police were here earlier. It can't be accidental. You were there hours after the shop closed. And it's nine o'clock in the morning, which means the shop should be open. Instead, there is a fire that has completely destroyed it. Now, as soon as the fire department is done, I'm sure we're going to find a body. And I have a very good idea who the victim is."

"I get it," said Terry. "You think the killer is trying up loose ends."

"Yes, I do," Marshall answered. "What's worse is you may have become a loose end. That means he may be coming after you."

"But how would he know?" asked Diana. "How did the killer know that the shop owner was a loose end now? Why now and not right after fixing the killer's car?"

"That's a good question," said Marshall. "Right now, the best thing is for you both to return to the newspaper office in case he calls."

"You think he'll call," Terry said staring at the remains of the smoldering building. "He calls after he kills some young girl, and it's to get us to find the body so that we will print a story. We already found the crime and are already reporting it. Why call?"

"Because this guy is demented, and he enjoys the attention," Marshall stated.

Terry and Diana realized they weren't going to find out anything at the scene. They took Marshall's advice and left. Freedman and Steven were at the newspaper office waiting when Terry and Diana returned. Freedman was on his cell phone. Steven was reading yesterday's paper.

"Has he called?" Terry asked Steven.

Steven put down the paper. "No, he hasn't."

Freedman finished his call. "That was Marshall," he said pointing to Terry. "He said to tell you they did find the body of the owner of the shop. He also said to expect a call from our mutual friend."

Right on cue, the phone rang. Terry waited for Steven to start the machine before answering the phone. "*City Times*, Editing."

"Saw you on TV," the voice said. "Who was that sweet thing with you? You got a girlfriend Terry?"

Terry felt his back shiver. "I don't know who you're talking about. Where did you see me?"

Steven gave Terry a thumbs-up to encourage him to keep the caller on the line.

"At the fire, don't you just love the live coverage TV has nowadays," the voice answered. "She was standing next to you. So, who is she?"

"I think you're talking about another reporter for some other newspaper. I really don't know who you are talking about. There were so many others there. Everyone was out there. It's what we do, report the news."

"Terry, you're lying. You know who I'm talking about. But don't worry, I'm not mad. I'll be in touch." The voice hung up.

"Did you get him?" Terry shouted still holding the phone in his hand.

"Sorry, but no. He wasn't on long enough."

Chapter Fourteen

Working for a daily newspaper is a constant rush to make the deadline. Papers have become more and more dependent on up-to-date, in-depth news stories, focusing on the local scene with the Internet covering national and international news. Television has less than twenty-two minutes to cover everything, including the weather, sports, and traffic. But newspapers have limited space, forty percent of which must carry advertising to cover the costs of producing the paper. Between finding and writing interesting stories, selling ads, and keeping up with the daily information such as TV listings; the editorial office is busy from the moment reporters come in to the final layout, beating the deadline necessary to print and deliver it on time. That all came to a standstill when Terry's phone rang an hour before deadline.

Because of the call that morning, the police had left for the day. Terry cursed himself; he still hadn't learned how to operate the machine to record and trace the call. He let it ring for the third time before answering it.

"What took you so long," demanded the voice.

"I was away from my desk," Terry answered. "I didn't expect you to call me twice in one day."

"Well, who said I was limited to just one phone call a day? Maybe I'm busy and have more stories for you."

"Look, have I upset you?" Terry asked, hoping somehow, he could elicit some kind of clue.

"It's a good thing I'm beginning to like you Terry."

"Why is that?"

"Why? Because I have another story for you. I hope you

like the movies. I'm a big fan of the old Alfred Hitchcock movies." The voice hung up without waiting for Terry's response.

"Crap," Terry said, hanging up the phone. "Carl, I need you to finish up for me."

Terry pulled up the local theater listing from his computer. He found a theater showing the Hitchcock movie *Psycho*. How appropriate Terry thought as he picked up the phone to call the police.

~ ~ ~

Terry met Detectives Marshall and Freedman at the entrance of the movie theater. Terry noticed several patrol officers standing at the exits. He was sure the killer had already left; still he was relieved to see them. Freedman showed the ticket seller his badge, which gained them entry to the theater. The manager of the theater objected to stopping the movie and bringing up the house lights. Marshall persuaded him to cooperate or face several visits from various public agencies to ensure there were no health code violations. The detectives and two patrol officers entered the theater as the house lights came on.

Marshall walked to the front of the screen and raised his hands. "Everyone, I'm Detective Marshall with the police department. We need your cooperation. Hopefully, it will only be a few minutes, and then the movie can continue. Could everyone stay seated and raise your hand?"

With the house lights on, Terry could see there were about thirty people in the audience. Everyone raised their hands, all except for one lady seated in the fourth row from the back. Freedman approached the woman. He nodded to Marshall.

Marshall signaled to the audience to put their hands down. "Sorry ladies and gentlemen. It seems this interruption is going to be longer than we hoped. Please remain seated until an officer gets your information. After that, we will need everyone to step into the lobby and wait."

"Why should we?" a woman sitting in the middle of the theater demanded. "You came into here and ruined the movie. Why should we do anything for you?" Several other patrons murmured agreement.

Marshall sighed heavily. Terry could tell Marshall didn't want to tell the real reason and upset the audience, but he really had no choice. "Ladies and gentlemen, a serious crime has been committed here. We need your cooperation with the investigation."

"What happened?" a man a few rows behind the first woman asked.

The patrol officers were moving from person to person, checking their identification and getting their contact information. But most of the attention was focused on Marshall. "There has been a homicide," he answered.

The patrons looked around, asked questions of each other, and several began to stand up.

"Sit down," Marshall ordered. "This is a police investigation. I need everyone here to do as I asked. I realize it's a great inconvenience. But someone was just murdered; and that person deserves all the help you can give her. Now, everyone, remain seated until a patrol officer gets your information. Then go and wait in the lobby. Myself, and Detective Freedman, will interview you."

"Are we under arrest?" The woman who had asked the first question, again demanded an answer.

"You are being detained in the course of a police investigation," Marshall replied as he walked to back of the theater and the exit to the lobby.

It took the patrol officers about twenty minutes to get everyone's information. One by one, Marshall and Freedman questioned each patron as he or she came into the lobby. While each patron had walked passed the victim, still seated in her seat, no one knew her or had any information about any person accosting her. Meanwhile, the crime scene technicians arrived and started looking for evidence. While the movie-goers were permitted to leave after talking to the detectives, most of them remained in the lobby, anxiously waiting for some news about the crime or for the coroner to bring out the body. Terry was sure several of the patrons regretted being so absorbed in the movie to miss a real homicide happening a few yards from them. Terry also noticed the media outside of the theater, and many from the audience were happy to give interviews.

Terry went up to Marshall. "I think I'll go back to the paper. I'm really not doing anything here except for being in the way."

"Don't think like that," Marshall said. "You led us here to the fifth victim. But you are right. It would be better for you to go back to your office in case the killer calls again. I'll have Steven meet you there. And, as soon as I get through here, I'll stop by and get a statement from you, so write down anything you can remember about the call."

Terry took a taxi back to the paper and met Steven, who was waiting for him. Terry made it a point to have Steven show him how to use the machine so that he could record any phone calls coming in.

Terry returned to his desk but didn't turn on his computer. He picked up the photograph from his desk. "Kristen, what can I do? There's a psycho out there killing people. It's a game to him. How can I stop him?"

Diana tapped Terry on the shoulder. "You miss her."

"She was someone I could talk to about work and problems. No matter how bad things got, she was there to support me. I could really use her help now."

"Why don't we go to Murphy's for a drink after work?"

"No, thanks," Terry answered.

"Seriously, I think it would do us good to talk about what you are going through. Hey, call your friend Paula and have her join us. We can brainstorm on ways to get this guy."

"I don't know."

"Terry, if you don't come, all you are going to do is go home and mope. You're going to sit in front of the TV and talk to pictures of Kristen. At least this way, we can try to do something. I'm sure Kristen would agree with me, sitting at home is not going to catch this killer."

~ ~ ~

Paula was sipping whiskey waiting for them when they arrived at Murphy's. Terry meekly raised his hand as a greeting and pulled out a chair. Diana signaled for a waitress to come over to take their order.

"Beer," Terry said without looking up. He fiddled with a coaster on the table.

"Gin and tonic for me," Diana said to the waitress. She turned to Paula. "What do you want?"

"I got it," was her reply.

"My goodness, you guys are ready to party," the waitress said teasingly. She inhaled deeply. "Seriously guys. Are you okay? You all seem down in the dumps."

"Thanks for asking," Diana replied. "We are, but it's not your fault. Please forgive us."

"Hey, it's all right," the waitress answered. "Just hate to see people having a hard time. Let me get you your drinks, and I'll bring over some popcorn for you all."

"Thank you," Diana said smiling at the young woman as she left.

The three of them sat in silence until the waitress returned with their drinks and a basket of popcorn. "That will be seven fifty. Will there be anything else for you?"

Diana gave the waitress a ten-dollar bill. "No, thank you. Not at this time. Keep the change."

"Why thank you. If you need anything else, just let me know." The waitress smiled as she left.

"Well, now that we've established we aren't here to

celebrate," Paula said. "Why are we here?"

"There was another murder today, actually two," Terry said, still fiddling with the coaster on the table. "One was a woman killed in a movie theater, in the middle of a matinee, with dozens of people around, but no one saw anything."

"You said there were two."

Diana lifted her drink and took a sip. "The shop owner of that body shop, the one we burglarized, there was a fire there this morning. After the fire department put out the flames, the police found the body of the shop owner."

"I'm beginning to think we'll never catch him," Terry moaned

"No, we'll catch him," Diana replied.

"She's right," Paula said while grabbing a handful of popcorn. "The question is when and how many people he'll kill before we get him."

"Stop," Diana said loudly, pounding the table with her palm. "Let's look at this logically. Let's think about what we know about him. Certainly, we can come up some ideas on how to catch him. Think! What do we know about him?"

"He's psycho," Terry said throwing the coaster on the table.

"No, she right," Paula responded. "Let's look at the murders. We know two of them, Kelly's and the one today, were done in daytime, during normal working hours. We know the one at the fairgrounds was done in the evening. We don't know when the others were done, but they had to be done either during daytime or in the evening, not late at night or early in the morning."

"How do you know that?" Diana asked.

"The way they were dressed," Paula answered. "The victims were wearing regular clothes. With the exception for the victim at the fairgrounds, none of the victims looked like they were dressing up for a date or had ran out of the house in the middle of the night to get something at a convenience store. Of course, that's just the impression I got from their clothes."

Diana nodded her head in agreement.

Paula picked up the coaster Terry had thrown on the table and pointed it at him. "So what kind of job does someone have that gives him time off during the day and in the evening?"

Again, Diana pounded the table with her hand. "So, he works nights."

Paula took another handful of popcorn. "I doubt it. People who work nights tend to keep a schedule. If that were the case, all of the killings would take place about the same time of the day. No, he can set his own schedule."

"So, he's unemployed or works part-time and doesn't have much money," Terry said with a degree of uncertainty.

Again, Paula shook her head. "I doubt money is an issue for him. He didn't rob the victims. It's my guess he lives alone, maybe in a home he inherited, so he has no rent. He's smart, so I'm willing to bet he works from his home."

"He has to be charming to get close to his victims," Diana added.

"Could be," Paula said. "But the murder today was in a theater, so he could have snuck up on her. Kelly was a receptionist, so he only had to walk in the door and she would have come up to him. As for the others, we really don't know how he approached them. He could have ambushed them, jumped them as they walked by a bush or wall he was hidden behind."

"But we know he drives a blue pickup truck," Terry exclaimed. "And we have his address."

Paula took out her notebook. "No, we have the name and address of someone who drives a blue pickup. Whether he is the killer or not has yet to be determined. Still, there is nothing wrong with checking the guy out. I would still like to find the guy who hit my car."

"Do we know anything else about the killer?" Diana asked, taking a handful of popcorn.

"Other than he's psycho," Terry replied.

"Yes, we do," Paula answered. "This guy likes to kill. I saw in Iraq. Some of the people I came across seemed to enjoy the bloodshed. There's a dark side to all of us. Trust me, I know. Most of us go through life never really knowing that part of us, and that's good. This person has found it, and he enjoys it. To him, it's a game, especially since he always calls to tell Terry about the body and where to find it. He's upped the game with his clues in the Sherlock Holmes books."

Terry held up his hand. "He didn't call with a clue about this last one."

Paula waved her hand. "He hasn't called yet. He will."

"So, you think he really is angry about wealthy people and those with pampered lives?" Diana questioned.

"No, it's a smoke screen," Paula answered. "Kelly wasn't rich, and she didn't have a pampered life. I'm sure if you check out the other victims, you'll find the same thing for most of them. I'm positive they were victims of opportunity."

"Anything else?" Terry asked.

Paula munched on some popcorn, giving her time to respond. "Here's what I suggest. Terry, you know the detectives handling the case. See if you can't get copies of the autopsy reports. Diana, you check out the victims. See if any of them had any kind of connection to any of the others, especially the ones before Kelly. Get as much as you can on their background. In the meantime, I'll focus on trying to find the guy with the truck. Let's meet back here tomorrow at the same time and see what we've found out."

Diana took a handful of popcorn and waved it at Paula. "Sounds like a plan."

Terry agreed. Even though they ordered more drinks, no one was celebrating.

Chapter Fifteen

The first thing Terry did the next morning was call Detective Marshall and ask for copies of the autopsy reports. Marshall said he would send them over by email later that morning. A few minutes later, Freedman and Steven arrived. Terry watched to be sure he knew how to use the machine recording his phone calls. Everyone continued to work, waiting for Terry's phone to ring.

"Special delivery," called out a voice loud enough to be heard throughout the office.

Everyone turned to see a young man in a FedEx uniform. "I have a special delivery for Mr. Terry Lambert. Is he here?"

Terry got out of his chair and approached the individual.

"Whoa, I didn't know I would have to deliver to midget."

"And what difference does that make?"

The delivery guy pointed to a line on the shipping label. "None, man. Just sign here."

Terry signed and took the package.

The delivery man put his pen in his pocket, then held out his hand. After a few seconds, he said, "Hey man, how about a tip?"

Terry looked up at the individual. "Here's your tip. Don't call short people midgets."

The delivery guy let his hand drop. He looked around, realizing everyone was staring at him. He waved and bowed slightly as he left the office.

Terry took the package to his desk and examined it before opening it. He pulled out a book, *The Hound of*

Baskervilles. Terry cautiously opened the book and flipped through the pages till he found a single sheet of paper.

> *Those who think they are exalted and high ranking because they were born to money need to learn not to abuse their power to oppress the middle class and the poor. Regardless of a person's position in society, everyone needs to be treated equally. The wealthy need to realize the real power is with the common people.*
>
> *The rich and wealthy use masks to hide their contempt and disgust of the true pillars of society. It is those without masks who are going to lead the world.*

Terry turned to Steven. "He's not going to call. Here's his message."

Freedman put on nitrile gloves and took the package, the book, and the note from Terry. "I doubt we will find any prints, but I'll have the lab process these."

Terry turned back to his desk and pounded it with his fist. "Damn it. This guy is toying with us. It's a game to him, and he's winning."

Diana came over and put her hand on Terry's shoulder. "Calm down. Let's focus on what we decided to do last night. Have you got the autopsy reports yet?"

"No, not yet. Detective Marshall said he would email them to me sometime this morning."

Diana gave Terry a brief hug. "Well then, in the meantime, just do your job. Don't let him get to you."

Terry nodded and sat down at his computer. The email from Marshall hadn't arrived yet. Terry pulled up the internet and typed in the titles of the three Sherlock Holmes novels. Terry was able to find brief synopsis of each book. The most interesting fact he discovered was *The Adventures of Sherlock Holmes* was the third book written by Sir Arthur Conan Doyle. *The Memoirs of Sherlock*

Holmes was the fourth book and *The Hound of Baskervilles* was the fifth.

Terry checked his email again, this time finding the autopsy reports Marshall had promised. The first victim was Frances Colton, a clerk at Walmart. She was stabbed more than a dozen times in her chest and abdomen. The time of her death was between twelve and sixteen hours before Terry had found her behind the abandon shopping center. The second victim was Emily Kemper, who was stabbed twice in the chest. Again, her death occurred between twelve and sixteen hours before her body was found. Joyce Youngblood was the third victim, again stabbed twice in the chest. Like the first two, death occurred between twelve to sixteen hours before the discovery of her body. For Kelly Richards, the fourth victim, and Denise Stebbins, the fifth one, in both cases the bodies were discovered less than an hour after they were stabbed. Kelly and Denise were stabbed twice in the chest, just like the other victims. All the victims, except Denise, showed signs of resistance and evidence of the killer physically overpowering them. However, there was one additional detail with Denise Stebbins. The coroner found bits of a leather glove in her teeth, meaning the killer wore leather gloves and put his hand over her mouth. Terry printed out the autopsy reports and went over to Diana.

Diana saw Terry approaching. She closed the file she was working on and opened up several others. "Glad you're here. Let me show you what I found." Terry came behind her to look over her shoulder.

Diana pointed to here screen. "Our first victim was Frances Colton, age 23, working at Walmart."

"Yeah, so?"

"She was also the second daughter of a very famous screenwriter in Hollywood. She was working at Walmart to learn about the retail business. She was following in her father's footsteps, trying to become a screenwriter."

"Okay."

"The next victim, the one you saw at the fairgrounds, was Emily Kemper, 25, and an intern at a local hospital. She had finished med school and was earning a whopping 60,000 dollars a year. Of course, who knows how much she would have made once she finished her internship. She was also engaged to a Navy lieutenant who is currently serving overseas. Then there is the third victim, Emily Youngblood, age 25, and an editor at a publishing house. She was also one fourth Cherokee. Again, not earning the big bucks."

"Interesting."

"Now for our last two victims, Kelly, Paula's friend, and Denise Stebbins, the woman at the movie theater. Kelly was a college student studying business administration. Denise was a homemaker. Her husband works at an automobile parts factory."

Terry crossed his arms and stared at the screen. "So, none of them were rich or famous."

"Well, the first victim, Frances, came from a wealthy family; but she wasn't. I'm sure Daddy paid whatever she couldn't afford, but she wasn't bringing in that much working at Walmart."

"So, you two are playing detective." Diana and Terry were startled by Steven who had come up behind them.

Terry looked around nervously. Diana stared up at Steven. "I do wish you wouldn't ease drop on private conversations," she said. "Isn't that a violation of the Fourth Amendment?"

Steven chuckled. "Nice try, but conversations in public places aren't protected if there is no expectation of privacy. Here in the middle of a newspaper office, hey come on."

"Look, we are just trying to find the killer," Terry said. "We thought if we looked into the victims, we might find some kind of motive or clue."

"Yeah, Marshall and Freedman thought the same thing," Steven answered. "They checked out the victimology of the first three victims. There were no connections. Look, you doing this is okay. If you find anything interesting, let me or the detectives know. But please limit yourselves to research on the computer. We don't want you getting hurt."

Diana looked at Terry, then Steven. "I promise you, if we find anything, you will be the first to know. We're reporters. We report the news. We don't want to become it."

~ ~ ~

Murphy's was crowded when Terry and Diana arrived. It took them a few minutes before they found Paula seated at a table. They joined her at the table.

"Well, good to see you again," said the same perky waitress from yesterday. "What can I get for you?"

Paula raised her glass to signal she already had a drink. Terry muttered for a beer and Diana ordered a gin and tonic.

"My goodness," the waitress commented as she took their order. "You all are still in dumps. Can today be as bad as yesterday?"

"You are really sweet to notice," Diana replied. "But things are really going bad for us at the moment. Please don't take it personally."

"It's not that. I just hate to see anyone having a bad day. Let me go and get you your drinks."

"Thanks," Terry mumbled as the waitress left. He watched her walk over to the bar before turning to Paula and Diana and placing a folder on the table. "Diana and I did some research and there is nothing to report, but I brought copies of the autopsy reports for you to see."

"Terry's right. There wasn't any kind of connection between the victims that we could find."

Paula opened the folder and spent several minutes going over each of the autopsy reports. Terry and Diana sat in silence.

Paula was still reading the reports when the waitress returned. "Here are your drinks. Also, I brought you some chips this time. I do hope things get better for you all."

Paula looked up from the papers in her hand and thanked her. After the waitress left, Paula leaned forward. Terry and Diana did the same.

"Did you notice the part about the stab wounds?" Paula asked.

Terry and Diana both shook their heads no.

"The first victim was stabbed multiple times, more than a dozen times. All of the other victims were stabbed only twice. Victims two, three, and four were stabbed in the chest, but only twice. Then there are the bruises that came when the victims tried to defend themselves. The fifth victim was in a movie theater, so he had to stab her in the chest, although he probably did it from the row behind the victim, so she didn't have time to resist. Still the only victim stabbed more than twice was the first victim, and she was stabbed repeatedly."

Terry gave Paula a look of confusion. "And that means. . .?"

Paula took a sip of her drink. "This is just a hunch, but I think the first murder victim and the killer knew each other. She was stabbed multiple times, which is sign of rage. It doesn't always mean that, but sometimes it does. The other victims were stabbed just twice. I think after the first murder, and the publicity he got from it, he enjoyed it and wanted it to continue. This is a game for him. He enjoys the killing and the attention he is getting."

"So, if we didn't print stories about the murders, he would stop," Terry said waving a potato chip to emphasis his point.

Paula gave him a don't-be-foolish look. "Yeah like that's going to happen. It doesn't matter if you print it or not. By now, he's famous and every other paper and TV station will cover any act he commits. He could fart in a crowded elevator and it would be on the six o'clock news."

"So, what does this mean," Diana asked.

"If he knew the first victim, then the others are red herrings," Paula explained, "killings designed to confuse the police and lead them in a different direction. The clues he leaves, just another way to get attention. The key is to focus on the first murder. Find out who would want to kill the first victim, Frances Colton."

"Also," Paula continued, "for the first three victims, he waited until the next day to call. For the last two, he called right afterwards. He's upping the game, taunting us to catch him."

"Again, what does that mean?" Diana asked.

"He's getting more dangerous."

"Hey, what about the guy with the pickup truck?" Terry said excitedly. "If we could prove a connection between him and the victim, then we will have our killer."

"Dead end," Paula said, "literally a dead end. I went to the address on the form we found at the body shop. Turns out the person whose name is on the form, Daniel Kuntz, died four months ago. I talked to his widow and it turns out he didn't, and never did, own a pickup truck."

"So, how do we check out the first victim?" Diana asked. "According to the research I did, her family is in California."

"But she worked here," Paula replied. "Do you know why she was working here and not in California?"

"No, I don't," was Diana's response.

Paula drained her drink. "Then let's find out."

~ ~ ~

If a dwarf, a tall blond, and pretty brunette walking in together was out of the ordinary, especially at nine o'clock in the evening, the Walmart greeter gave no indication. It wasn't till the trio stopped in front of Frances Colton's picture did the middle-aged woman wearing a blue vest with Walmart's logo on it say anything.

"It was so tragic," the greeter said. "She was killed a few weeks ago, and such a lovely girl."

Diana touched the woman's arm. "I'm sure she was. Would it be possible to talk to the manager?"

"Well, yes. But maybe I can help you."

"Would prefer to talk to the manager, if you don't mind," Paula said to the woman.

The greeter stared at Paula. "Well, I'll go get her. Please wait here." Less than two minutes later she returned, followed by slender African-American woman, also wearing a blue vest.

"I'm Marion Dempsey, the manager. Can I help you?"

Terry, Paula, and Diana looked at each other. Diana decided to take the lead and ask the questions. "I'm Diana Hawley. I work for the *City Times*. I was hoping you could tell me a little bit about Frances. I know she was murdered, but I would really like to know what kind of person she was, who her friends were, etc. You know, her life here at Walmart."

The manager put her hand to her lips and took a deep breath. "Well, I'll tell you," she said taking her hand away from her mouth, "Frances was a real sweetheart. Always friendly, and well liked. Her murder was a shock to us all. We are all still grieving from her death. I didn't know her that well, but perhaps Joseph, who worked with her could answer your questions better. Wait here and I'll page him."

The manager returned to her office. A minute later they could hear Joseph being paged. Terry, Paula, and Diana waited uncomfortably under the watchful eye of the Walmart greeter who stared at them between smiling at customers coming into the store. Relief came when a young man who needed a shave, also in a blue vest, came up to the group.

"Heard there were some people from the paper here," he said extending his hand to each of them in turn. "I'm Joseph Simms. What can I do for you?"

Again, Diana accepted the role of spokesperson. "Can you tell us about Frances?"

"Sure," Billy answered. "What do you want to know?"

Diana gestured with her hands. "Who were her friends? What did she do here? Did she have any problems with anyone?"

"Man, you sound like the police," Joseph said. "They asked the same questions when they were here. Let me see. She worked with me in the electronics section. She was really sharp, especially about computers and the software. Everyone liked her; I mean she was nice to everybody. I never heard of her having any problems here. I know she liked movies. She really like the older ones from the like the 40's, 50's, etc. She was really into suspense and mysteries like Hitchcock, Phillip Marlowe, The Thin Man series, Sherlock Holmes, Sam Spade, Boston Blackie, and so forth."

"I understand she was from California," Paula said. "Do you know what brought her out here?"

"I heard she came here for college, but I know she wasn't attending school when she worked here."

"Do you know which school?" Paula asked.

"Sorry, no."

"One last question," Paula said. "Did Frances have any kind of conflict with anyone, either here or outside of work?"

"I wouldn't know about outside of work," Joseph answered, "You would have to ask her boyfriend, but here, there were no problems."

Diana let out a small gasp. "She had a boyfriend?"

"I think so," Joseph answered. "I saw someone pick her up a couple of times."

"Can you describe him," Paula asked.

"You sound just like the police," Joseph said with a slight giggle. "Didn't really get to see him. I know it was some white dude who drove a pickup truck, but that's all."

Terry held up his hand. "What color was the pickup?"

"Blue."

Chapter Sixteen

Paula truly appreciated Walmart being open 24 hours a day. After talking to Joseph, Paula realized she needed to get some groceries. She grabbed a shopping cart and began strolling aisles, picking up mostly canned or ready to eat meals. The only time she really stopped to examine the products on the shelves was when she found the liquor section. After several minutes of examining the selection on the shelves, she realized they sold only beer and wine. For the hard stuff, she would have to stop by a liquor store.

Something, a strange tingling in the back of neck, the kind of sensation that kept her alive in Iraq, made Paula look around the parking lot as she placed her purchases in the back seat of her car. She got in her car and pulled out of the lot, taking care to notice which cars followed her. There was a white sedan behind her. Paula continued down the road, stopping at a late-night liquor store to pick up two bottles of Jim Beam. When Paula came out of the store, she noticed a white sedan parked across the street. She knew there were lots of white sedans on the road, but this one spooked her. She pulled out of the parking lot, made three quick right turns, and two lefts before heading home. Fifteen minutes later she pulled into the parking lot of her apartment complex. A white sedan was parked in front of her apartment building. Paula reached into the glove box and pulled out her nine-millimeter automatic.

"You almost lost me," said the man getting out of the vehicle. It took a moment for Paula to recognize the person as Ashford.

"You're lucky I didn't shoot you," Paula replied as she placed her weapon in the small of her back and began to gather her groceries from her car.

Ashford rushed up to her. "Here let me help you with that."

"Oh, you're such a gentleman," Paula said sarcastically.

"Always willing to help a damsel in distress."

"Well this damsel was about to put you in distress. Why are you following me?"

"Saw you with Terry and Diana earlier. Kind of wondered what you were up to. I hung back until the other two left. I was going to approach you in Walmart, but I lost you when I went to get a shopping cart. By the time I found you, you were checking out. Figured you were coming home until I saw your car at a liquor store. Then, you took off and made all those turns. Traffic kept me from keeping up with you. So, I headed back here and got lucky. I found you."

"Didn't know I was lost."

"Awe, come on," Ashford pleaded. "I'm just concerned about you. That's all."

Paula handed Ashford the bag containing the whiskey. "So, you followed me around, made me nervous, and almost got yourself shot. You really have no idea how lucky you really were. Now, be careful with that. I'm trusting you with the most important purchase I've made all week."

"Then I can come in?"

Paula knew she should send Ashford away. She was angry knowing how close she had come to hurting him. She knew he was just interested in using her to get information for his next article. That was okay. She was going to use him too.

~ ~ ~

Paula sighed heavily as she sipped her morning coffee. Ashford was still asleep. Paula thought about making something for breakfast. She had groceries from last night, but her heart wasn't in it. She walked into the bedroom and gently kicked Ashford's sleeping form.

"Get up," she commanded. "You'll be late for work."

"What time is it?" a sleepy Ashford asked.

"Time for you to get up and go to work."

Ashford grinned. "Come on, don't be like that. We had a good time last night."

Paula bent down and kissed his forehead. "Honey, it was great. Loved every moment. But now time's up, so get up."

"I've got to use the bathroom first," Ashford said as he dragged his naked body out of bed.

"You know where it is."

"So, what did you all find out about the killer last night?" he asked over his shoulder through the open door of the bathroom.

Paula smiled. She took a moment to contemplate whether she should tell him or not. Ashford was being a real dog about using her. She decided to throw him a bone. "Terry, Diana, and I think the killer drives a blue pickup truck."

"And?"

Paula took another sip of coffee before answering. "Call it a hunch, but I think the killings are a smoke screen for the first one. If the police can solve the first murder, they can catch this guy."

"So, what's the Walmart connection? Ashford asked as he exited the bathroom.

"There isn't any," Paula said smiling. She knew Ashford didn't believe her, but she wanted him to work for it. He would have to find out on his own.

"So what were you guys doing there?"

"Chasing a dead end. Now you get dressed."

"Well, what are you doing today?"

Paula turned away. She walked back into the kitchen and poured herself some more coffee. She was tempted to add some whiskey; but having whiskey for breakfast was a line she wasn't willing to cross.

A fully clothed Ashford came up behind her and put his hands on her arms. "Hey, you okay?"

Paula turned to face him. "Yeah, I'm okay. It's just that today is going to be a hard day."

"Why is that?"

Paula sniffled. "I have to help Kelly's family with her funeral arrangements."

"Oh, that's rough."

"No, what's rough is the son of a bitch who did this is still out there; and he's going to kill again."

~ ~ ~

"Good, you're here," Terry shouted as Marshall and Steven walked into the editorial office the next morning.

"Why, what happened?" Steven asked. "Did the killer call this morning?"

"No, but we found a clue to his identity."

"Not again," Marshall said with a groan.

"But we did," Terry insisted. "Last night, we went to Walmart, where the first victim, Frances Colton worked. It turns out she had a boyfriend; a boyfriend who drove a blue pickup truck."

Marshall sighed and stared at Terry. "We know about him. Unfortunately, we weren't able to locate him. After the second victim, we moved on. Why would the boyfriend kill all of the other women?"

Diana was leaning against her desk. "Good question. Paula, the person we were with when we got arrested, thinks this guy likes killing. She thinks the first killing was motivated by jealousy or something. But the guy discovered he liked it. When he started getting press coverage, he loved the attention. In other words, there was a motive for the first murder. The others were people in the wrong place at the wrong time."

"You have a good point," Marshall said. "We checked out the boyfriend angle, but quickly lost interest in it when other victims began to show up. It wasn't until you brought up the blue pickup, that we renewed our interest in trying to locate the boyfriend."

Terry's face lit up with excitement. "So, the killer is the one driving the blue pickup. Did you check out the address we gave you?"

Marshall sat down at a desk near Terry's. "Yes, we checked it out. The address was for a Daniel Kuntz, deceased, and he never owned a pickup."

"Yeah, we know," Diana said.

"Still, this mysterious blue pickup is a solid lead," Marshall continued. "The boyfriend of the first victim drove one. There was one seen at the scene of the second murder. Then there was the incident with you being run off the road. These are too much to be coincidence. Unfortunately, there are a lot of blue pickup trucks on the road. We need some other way to narrow down the field."

What do you mean?" Terry shouted. "It has a damaged passenger side from ramming us and there's a bullet hole in the tailgate. There can't be many blue pickups matching that description."

"You're right about that," Marshall conceded. "But, unless it's on the road, we won't find it. I'm pretty sure the killer is using a different car now. He probably has the pickup stored somewhere. If he paints it, then it will be even harder to find him."

"So, what do we do?" Diana asked.

"We wait and hope for a break," Marshall answered.

~ ~ ~

For the third consecutive night, Diana and Terry met Paula at Murphy's. Again, the perky waitress was disappointed when she greeted them. "Do you guys ever have a good time," she asked. "I mean you come in here, always depressed."

Paula sighed. "Look, whether we're happy or depressed isn't your business. Your job is to serve us drinks and bring us whatever food we order. Yes, we're having a bad week. Get over it and focus on your job."

"Paula," Diana whispered. "She's trying to cheer us up. Don't treat her like that just because you're angry."

"Stuff it," Paula replied. "I'll treat her any way I want."

"No, you won't," Terry answered. "She doesn't deserve that." He turned to the young woman. "Please forgive us, but we are having a rough time. You haven't done anything wrong. Please bring me a beer. Diana, what will you have?"

"Gin and tonic. Paula?"

"Whiskey, neat."

"Okay," the waitress replied. "I'll be right back with your drinks."

As soon as she left, Diana turned to Paula. "What is your problem? That waitress didn't deserve to be treated that way."

"Shut up."

"No," Terry said. "Diana's right. You can't take your anger out on her. It's not her fault. Now, what's wrong?"

The waitress returned, placed their drinks on the table. "Will there be anything else?" she asked obviously annoyed.

"Yes," Terry answered. "What is your name?"

"Becky," she replied cautiously.

"Well Becky, I want to apologize for our behavior earlier. Just know you did nothing wrong."

The waitress looked around. She pulled up the empty chair and sat down. "Look, I see all kinds in here. I just hate to see you all always so depressed."

Paula reached out and patted Becky's hand. "Thank you, sweetheart. Terry's right. I shouldn't take out my frustrations on you."

"Well, what's wrong? Why are you all depressed?"

"We're going through a rough patch," Diana answered.

Becky turned to Paula. "Why are you so depressed?"

Paula looked down at her glass, avoiding eye contact. "A funeral. A friend of mine was murdered last week. I spent the day with her family helping them with her funeral arrangements for tomorrow."

"Sorry to hear that," Becky said.

"Thank you."

Terry twirled his mug of beer around on the coaster. "You dealt with the deaths of friends and funerals when you were in the service."

"You were in the service?" Becky asked.

"Yeah. Marines. And yes, I've dealt with funerals and deaths of friends. It never got easier."

Becky came around behind Paula and gave her a gentle hug. "Thank you for your service." Becky faced the bar. "Hey, Tommy, I'm taking a break."

Becky set her tray on the table and sat in the empty chair next to Paula. "Look I know it's hard to lose someone. I lost my cousin in Afghanistan four years ago. Our family is close, so losing anyone hurts."

"Sorry for your loss," Paula meekly replied.

Becky put her hand on Paula's. "Thank you, but this isn't about who loss who. I hated it when at my cousin's funeral everyone was trying to tell his family about how they loss someone and how time made things better. You know what made them feel better. When people came up, gave them a hug, and said they were there for them. What's important is to know people care about you and your friend. I understand your grief. Wish I could do more than say I cared. I do care, and I hope you find some solace in knowing your friends are here for you."

Paula downed her whiskey in a single gulp. "Damn it. I hate it when people are nice to you, especially after I treat them so badly."

Becky leaned over and gave Paula another hug. "Don't worry about it. Friends understand."

"We're friends?" Paula asked with surprise.

Becky got up and picked up her tray. "We are now," she said as she walked away to take care of other customers.

Paula watched Becky as she walked away. "That girl's nuts." Paula smiled. "I like her."

Terry and Diana returned Paula's smile and raised their glasses in a silent toast.

Chapter Seventeen

The nice thing about funeral homes is that so many *people came, no one knows everyone,* he thought as he entered. He had shaved his beard and made sure to wear a nice suit. He also got a haircut, so his hair was much shorter than before. To add to his disguise, he wore glasses with a dark plastic frame. The lens were plain glass, but no one would notice. He found a spot where he was out of the way, but could observe all those who came in. He smiled to himself when he saw the tall blond woman, the dwarf, and the pretty brunette walk into the funeral home. Then he remembered the blond woman had a pistol, and she had put a hole in the tailgate of his truck. He made a mental note not to get too close to her during the service.

~ ~ ~

Terry noticed two things about Paula on this day. One, she wasn't sad, she was vengeful. He could tell she wanted to find the man who had killed Kelly. Terry imagined Paula would gleefully attend his funeral. The second thing was Paula looked like a professional business woman in her black pants suit. When she was not wearing gym clothes or jeans, she was an attractive woman. Terry also noted Diana was looked quite attractive in her black dress with a pearl necklace and earrings.

They approached the registration table. An attractive young woman pointed to a computer. The three of them stood there for a moment, wondering what to do.

"Oh, this is the latest thing," a voice behind them said. They turned to see Becky. The perky waitress as wearing a black mini skirt, white blouse, and a dark jacket.

"Huh, nice to see you," Paula said. "What are you doing here? Did you know Kelly?"

"No," Becky answered. "I know you. I came to give you all support. I was serious when I said friends care about friends, especially when they are going through a hard time."

"Did we tell you about the funeral?" Paula asked.

"No, but the paper did. It listed your friend's name and her cause of death, as well as details about her funeral. So, I hope you don't mind, but it seemed you all need all of the support you can get,"

"How sweet of you," Diana replied. "So, what were you saying?"

"The computer," Becky answered pointing to the keyboard. "Funeral homes are having people sign in using a computer instead of having them sign in a guest book. They then send the list to the family. Also, I'm sure they use it for marketing." Becky moved between them, to the keyboard. "See, you type in your name, address, phone number, and email address. Now, the family knows who was here."

Paula, Terry, and Diana followed Becky's instructions. The four of them went into the main sanctuary. Paula whispered to Terry, "This girl is nuts. We meet her in a bar and she shows up here, at a funeral for someone she doesn't know. Something's not right."

"Probably not," Terry whispered back. "But she's not causing a problem, so I would let it go for now."

They all sat down in a middle row. "Is that the family in the front row on the left?" Becky asked. "We want to be sure to give them our condolences after the service."

"Yes," Paula answered. "I spent most of yesterday with them. I'm sure they are going to appreciate your support."

Becky leaned over to whisper to Paula. "By the way, I

know I'm a bit strange, but you really have nothing to fear from me. Even though I didn't know the deceased, I'm here to support you."

"It's just that it's unusual," Paula replied.

"I prefer to think of it as eccentric."

~ ~ ~

He watched intently. The perky young blond was a surprise. *Terry, did you find me my next victim* he thought. *How nice of you.* The service was full of people telling their stories about the young woman in the coffin. He took special interest when the tall blond got up to tell her story. The blond informed the audience and the family the police were making progress in the case and they would catch the killer in the near future. It was an added bonus that she would include him in the service, although he had no fear of being caught or recognized here. Still, when the service ended, and people passed the coffin to bid the young woman farewell and to offer their condolences to the family, he quietly retreated. He didn't want to press his luck. He was waiting in a van when the tall blond, the dwarf, and the two young ladies came out. First the dwarf and the brunette left. That left the two blonds. One of them got into an old VW bug. He smiled as he started his van.

~ ~ ~

Paula said good bye to Terry and Diana as they left the funeral. She knew they had to return to work. Becky gave Terry and Diana a hug as they left.

Becky faced Paula. "I hope I didn't upset you by coming today."

"It was unexpected, but appreciated," Paula replied. "Kelly would have liked you. I wish you had gotten a chance to know her."

"So do I," Becky said as she hug Paula. "Sorry, but I have to go to work. Will you be okay?"

Paula smiled. "Yeah, I'll be okay. Thanks for coming."

Paula watched as Becky got into her vintage Volkswagen Bug. Paula failed to notice the van following Becky's vehicle.

~ ~ ~

It was becoming a regular habit. Paula, Terry, and Diana meeting at Murphy's for a drink after work. Becky was as perky as ever when she came over with their drinks.

"We haven't ordered yet," Diana said as Becky placed the drinks on the table.

"You always order the same thing: whiskey for Paula, a beer for Terry, and a gin and tonic for you. And I brought you some popcorn. It's free, the popcorn is; you still have to pay for the drinks."

"Here," Paula said handing Becky a ten-dollar bill. "Keep the change. And by the way, thanks again for coming today."

"Hey, we're friends. And that's what friends do." Becky left to take care of the bill.

Paula lifted up her glass and waved in the direction of waitress. "That girl is about as mentally stable as a two-legged chair. And I bet if I told her that, she would think it was a compliment."

"I think she's a sweetheart," Diana said, glancing over her shoulder to catch a glimpse of Becky at the bar.

"What are you going to do," Terry asked. "Is the gym going to open back up?"

"Yeah," Paula answered. "They'll open back up tomorrow. I don't expect many people for the first couple of days. Still, I'll be there working out in case anyone wants some coaching."

"You're not going to look for the blue pickup anymore?" Terry asked. "The killer is still out there."

Paula took a final gulp of her drink. She raised her glass to signal Becky for another one. "The police are looking for the pickup and they're going to have better luck than I am in finding it. I checked out the address we got from the body shop. It was a dead end, literally, the guy who lived there had died."

"Wait a minute, wait a minute," an excited Diana said. "How did the killer know the address of some dead guy?"

"I don't get you," said Paula. "He probably read in a newspaper or something."

"No," Diana said stabbing the table with her finger. "I started out in obituaries. I remember only one obituary. It was someone I had gone to high school with."

"So, a person you knew died,"

"You're missing the point," Diana said throwing her hands out in front of her. "The only one I remembered was the one of a person I knew. I'm willing to bet the reason the killer gave the body shop owner that fake name and address was because he knew the person, and he knew the person was dead."

"And how does that help us?" Paula asked.

Becky returned with a whiskey for Paula. "Anyone want anything else?"

"Becky," Diana said so forcibly that it startled the waitress. "You told us this afternoon that funeral homes keep electronic records of guests for funerals."

"Well," Becky said drawing out the word. "Some funeral homes now have computer sign-ins. It's easier for them to keep a record of all the guests. Afterwards, they provide the family with the list. One advantage is you can read everyone's name; no trying to decipher someone's handwriting. Sometimes, they use the lists for their marketing."

"I got it," Terry exclaimed. "We go to the funeral home where this guy had his funeral and get the list. Then we check each name until we find the killer."

"Great idea there, Sherlock," Paula sarcastically replied. "How are we going to find a killer when we don't know what he looks like?"

"We know he drives a blue pickup," Terry answered. "And please don't remind of Sherlock Holmes."

"Why not?" Becky asked. "He was a great detective."

"The killer keeps leaving clues in Sherlock Holmes mysteries."

"Which ones?"

Terry looked up at Becky. "He started with the third homicide. He left a note in a book titled *The Adventures of Sherlock Holmes*. For the fourth murder, he left a note in *The Memoirs of Sherlock Holmes*. The last one was Kelly, the person the funeral was for today. For this one, he left a note in *The Hound of Baskervilles*."

"Seriously," Becky questioned. "He left a note in *The Adventures of Sherlock Holmes* for the third murder, a note in *The Memoirs of Sherlock Holmes* for the fourth murder, and a note in *The Hound of Baskervilles* for the fifth murder. That's a clue."

Terry glanced at Paula and Diana before placing his mug of beer on the table and staring at Becky. "Come again?"

"It's a clue," an excited Becky said waving her arms. "The note for the third murder was in the third novel about Sherlock Holmes, the fourth clue was in the fourth book, and the fifth clue was in the fifth book. Each clue correlates to the book in the same order as the murder."

"Okay, I can see the connection, but I don't see how this can help us find the murderer," Terry responded.

"It means our killer is a Sherlock Holmes fan," Paula stated. "He's well read, educated, intelligent, and won't stop until he's committed a murder for each Sherlock Holmes novel. How many novels were there?"

"There were four novels," Becky answered. "But there were nine books published."

Diana swirled her drink. "You know a lot about Sherlock Holmes."

"My last name is Watson, like Dr. Watson, the character

in Sherlock Holmes stories. And my father is a doctor, well, a dermatologist, but still a doctor. So of course, I grew up reading them."

"You seem like a fairly intelligent girl," Terry said. "Why don't you go to college and get a better job."

"Hey, don't call me a girl. I'm 24-year-old college graduate with a BA in literature. That makes me an educated woman, not a girl. As for getting a job, believe it or not, you are looking at the job market for people with a degree in literature."

"Sorry, I didn't mean to offend you," Terry apologized.

"You got moxie," Paula said raising her glass to Becky.

"I work in a bar. I want to be friendly, but not that friendly. There are times when being sweet won't cut it."

"Have a seat," Diana said pulling out a chair for Becky.

Becky yelled over to the bar. "Tommy, taking a break."

"Here's what we know so far," Paula began explaining to Becky as she sat down. "Our killer uses a knife and he's very good with it. He likes killing. He seeks out young women, victims of opportunity. He's killed these victims at various times of the day, which makes it hard for us figure out his schedule. He could be wealthy and not need to work, unemployed and out of a job, a person who takes on odd jobs, whatever; we don't know. He's intelligent. He knows forensics. He hasn't left any physical evidence at any crime scene. He likes the attention he is getting from the media. He calls Terry whenever he kills someone, and he tells Terry where to find the body. He started calling about clues, statements he's made, and left as notes in books at various places, a library, a book store, etc. We have reason to believe he drives a blue pickup truck. He tried to run Terry and me off the road a couple of days ago, so his truck is pretty banged up on the passenger side. Also, there is a bullet hole in the tailgate. We think he's young, in his 20's or 30's, and medium build. We have no idea what his end game is."

Becky held her serving tray in her lap. "Aren't the police

looking for this guy?"

"Of course, they're looking," Terry replied. "It's just that we are trying to figure him out so that we can help the police."

"Do the police know everything you know?" Becky asked.

Diana took a sip from her drink. "Of course. We are working with them; we are holding nothing back. This is not about getting a news story. It's about stopping a killer."

Becky closed one eye and looked at Paula.

"What?" Paula asked forcefully.

Becky opened both eyes and leaned forward with her serving tray between her and the table. "This guy is smart. He knows literature, especially Sherlock Holmes literature. He knows police procedures. And the time of day doesn't matter, which means he has control of his own schedule."

Terry acknowledged Becky's statement with a nod of his head and a drawn-out okay.

Becky sat back, placed her serving tray on the table, and smiled. "You know the dream of every literature major is to write a book and get it published. Then we would get lots of money and meet lots of movie stars."

Paula gave Becky a frustrated look. "Great, here's to you writing the great American novel and winning the Nobel Prize. What does this have to do with our killer?"

Becky looked down at her hands. "What if he was an agent, one who specialized in murder mysteries?"

"And?" Paula said drawing out the word.

"If he were an agent, he would have control over his schedule. Most agents work from home and set their own hours. He would have access to lots of manuscripts that would describe how to commit a perfect crime. He would learn a lot about police procedures and how to avoid them."

"What would be his motivation for killing people?" Diana asked staring into her drink.

"Sorry. Haven't a clue," was Becky's answer.

Chapter Eighteen

"What the hell is this crap?" Ashford bellowed.

"Probably one of your stories," Terry mumbled just loud enough for Diana, seated a few feet away, to hear.

"Who wants coffee?" Steven shouted as he entered the editorial office. "We brought donuts and coffee for anyone who wants it."

"Great way to start the morning," Detective Freedman added, walking into the office.

"Forget the donuts," Ashford continued to bellow. I want to know who did this."

"Who did what?" Freedman asked.

"It's none of your business," Ashford shouted back. "You are supposed to come here, listen to the Runt's phone, and that's all. Besides, what is taking you so long to catch this guy?"

Steven busied himself with checking the recording machine. Freedman put down the box of donuts and walked over to Ashford, stopping a few feet from him. "I don't know what your problem is, but don't take it out on me, or anyone else. You're having a rough day. Too bad. Deal with it."

"Look you don't understand. I'm Ashford Zane, the top reporter for this rag. And this morning I come in to find out I have been assigned to cover the opening of a pet shelter fund raiser they're having at a supermarket. I don't cover these kinds of stories. Interns and reporter wantabes cover this, not me."

Freedman walked away. "Sorry, I don't deal with people with bruised egos."

"It's not a bruised ego," Ashford shouted.

"No ,it's arrogance, conceit, condescension, insolence, being self-centered; sorry, I'm running out of adjectives," Steven replied smugly.

"You don't understand; and you don't know what you're talking about," Ashford said jabbing his finger at Steven, who was across the room.

"That's right," Terry answered. "This is a case of where the assignment is easy and something we normal give to beginning reporters to give them experience."

"That's right," Ashford agreed adamantly.

"And in this case," Terry continued, "obviously this assignment is too demanding for him to handle."

Everyone in the editorial office giggled. The amusement ended when Terry's phone rang. Steven turned on his machine.

Terry took a deep breath before picking up his phone. "Good morning, *City Times*, copyediting."

"Terry, you don't sound happy to hear from me," the distorted voice at the other end said.

"You're calling to report another body."

"Terry, you're not looking at this in a positive way. I'm calling to give you a news story."

"You're calling to tell me you've killed another innocent victim."

"You need to learn to have more enthusiasm. You should go back to school. Try to recapture the enthusiasm kids had when they were in elementary school. That enthusiasm is central to learning. Bye Terry."

"Wait," Terry shouted into the phone, only to be answered by a dial tone.

Terry replaced the handset on the phone. "Great, now we have to figure out where he left the body."

Central Elementary School," Freedman said taking out his cell phone. "My kids go there. Today is a *teacher training day*, whatever that is. It means teachers are there, but kids aren't."

"How do you know that's what he meant?" Ashford demanded.

Freedman looked at Ashford. Several people in the office wondered if Freedman was going to shoot Ashford. They were also wondering if they should care if Ashford got shot or not. Those who didn't care seemed to be winning the competition. "He mentioned an elementary school, which is probably his clue to where the body is. Central Elementary is the closest school, so I suggest we start there."

"Now that's the story I should be covering," Ashford shouted.

Terry and Diana were following Freedman and Steven out the door. Ashford gathered up the information about the pet shelter and handed it to another reporter. "You tell Fitch to give that to someone else. I'm going to cover the homicide at the school."

Ashford ran down the stairs to see Terry and Diana get in the back of a police car. He watched the unit drive away with its lights and siren. Ashford held up his hand for a taxi, cursing each one that passed him. He was yelling obscenities at one taxi when another pulled up. Ashford grabbed the door handle before it could pull away, startling both the passenger getting out and the driver.

"Hurry, hurry," Ashford demanded of the man getting out of the taxi. The passenger paid his fare, along with a tip. When the passenger asked for a receipt, Ashford looked up at the sky and groaned. The taxi driver printed out the receipt and tore it off of the machine. Ashford grabbed it and thrust it to the passenger's hand before jumping in the cab.

"What's your problem," said the taxi driver, looking at Ashford through his rearview mirror.

"Cut the small talk," Ashford demanded. "I need you to

get me to Central Elementary School now."

The taxi driver continued to look at Ashford through the rearview mirror. "What's the hurry? You late for your kid's recital or something?"

"No, I'm not late. Never mind that, I don't have any kids. I need to get to Central Elementary; that's all you need to know. Now can you do it or not?"

"Man, you need to cut back on your caffeine intake. Yeah, I'll get you there." The driver put the taxi in gear and pulled away from the curb.

"Hurry," Ashford demanded.

"Hey man, you need to mellow out or I'm going to pull over and throw you out of my cab. I'll get you there as quickly as I can, depending on traffic."

Ashford held up two twenty-dollar bills. "Will this make you go any faster?"

"No," the driver answered emphatically. "What is your hurry anyway?"

"Not that it's any of your business, but I'm a reporter and a major news story is breaking over there right now. So, hurry."

The driver pulled the taxi to the curb and turned around in his seat to face Ashford. "You can learn some manners and be patient; or you can start walking to that school. Now I will get you there as quickly as I can, obeying all traffic laws. So, you can take those bills you are waving around and put them away. Now have I made myself clear, or do you need me to explain it again?'

Ashford put the bills back in wallet.

The driver waited a few seconds before turning back and pulling away from the curb. He continued to watch Ashford in the backseat. Ashford stared back. The driver was unimpressed.

Ashford continued to scowl the entire twenty minutes it took to get to the school. The driver pulled into the front of the building, then he saw the patrol vehicles by another entrance. He drove over to that entrance. "Here you are," he said, "your fare is eighteen seventy-five."

Ashford threw a twenty-dollar bill at the driver. "Keep the change." Ashford was out of the vehicle before the driver could respond.

Ashford bounded up the stairs. "Press," he announced to the patrol officer at the door.

The officer held up his hand. "Sorry sir, this is an active crime scene. I can't allow anyone in."

"I'm a member of the press. I demand access. Or haven't you ever heard of *Freedom of the Press*, which is guaranteed by our Constitution."

The patrol officer scoffed and turned his head. "Hey, Fred. We got a lawyer out here claiming Freedom of the Press," he said over his shoulder. "You want this one?"

"Sure, sounds like fun," said a patrol officer coming out of the building. He pointed to Ashford. "You the one claiming Freedom of the Press?"

Ashford inhaled to expand his chest. "That's right. I'm a member of the press and I demand access to the crime scene. The U.S. Constitution guarantees Freedom of the Press, which means I have a right to see what is going on in there."

"No, you don't," the patrol officer replied. "Freedom of the Press means you can print anything you want as long as it's accurate. It means you can criticize the government, government agencies, government officials, etc. without fear of reprisal. But nowhere does it say we have to give you access to an active crime scene. Now our job is to keep people out until the crime scene folks are done. So you can wait over there, or we can take you into custody and have you wait down at the station. Which one will it be?"

"No, don't give him a choice," Terry said emerging from inside the building. "Just shoot him."

The police officers chuckled. "Sorry, we can't do that," one of them answered. "If we shot all of people who behaved this rudely, we would run out of bullets."

"Wait a minute," Ashford demanded. "Why can he go inside, but I can't?"

"He's helping with the investigation," the officer stated.

"But we work for the same newspaper."

"And you still have to wait over there," the officer said pointing to a shaded area under a tree near a curb.

Ashford continued to scowl at Terry as he walked to area the police officer pointed. Terry simply grinned and waved his fingers to him before going back inside.

~ ~ ~

He chuckled to himself as he watched the scene from his van. *What a jerk* he thought watching the one guy, who he assumed was some kind of reporter make a fool of himself demanding to go into the school. He could tell the reporter and Terry had some kind of disagreement. He was pleased that Terry had shown up along with that attractive brunette. He realized he should have selected a victim on the side of the building facing the street. That way he could see what the police were doing. But the victim he needed worked on the other side.

This one had been different. It would mess up any patterns the police had. He told the teacher he was the father of one her students. She didn't believe him and wouldn't let him in the room. She kept him at the door. He realized he wouldn't be able to bluff his way in, so he pushed the door open. She turned to run, but he grabbed her and stabbed her twice. She tried to stop him, even grabbing his arm, but it didn't help her. She had held on tight, and it took several minutes before she bled out and her hand fell from his sleeve.

He wondered, should he wait until they bring the body out? He was lost in thought when he heard a knocking on the rear window of the car.

"Hey, buddy. Need you to move along. You can't hang around here."

He silently cursed himself. He had been paying too much attention to what was going on across the street to notice the police officer approaching his car. "Is there a problem, officer," he asked.

"No, no problem. Just that we have a situation and we want to keep the area clear of traffic. Just need you to move along."

"Certainly, officer. Anything to oblige." It was a disappointment that he wouldn't see them bring out the body. But it couldn't be helped.

~ ~ ~

Terry walked back to join Diana. A patrol officer signaled for them to remain outside of the classroom. They watch Steven, Detectives Marshall and Freedom carefully place yellow plastic numbered markers around the body. Some marked blood, one was for a piece of cloth, and others were for possible clues. Marshall came out of the classroom.

"Do you want to know about the victim?" he asked.

Terry pulled out his notebook. "Sure, go ahead."

"As you can see, she's an African-American. According to her driver's license, her name is Sheila Dunning, age 26. The principal told me she was married, but he didn't know if she had any kids. I have a patrol going to the husband's workplace to inform him. He's a manager of self-storage unit."

"Hey detective," Steven shouted. "We just got lucky. We found some physical evidence linked to the killer." Steven walked over to them with his camera and brought a digital photo up in the viewfinder. "Here is a button and a piece of the shirt the killer was wearing. We found it in her hand. And, we found a partial footprint, in blood, so we know it was the killer's."

"He's getting sloppy," Terry said trying to see the photos on the back of the camera. Steven realized Terry was shorter than everyone else, and he lowered the camera to show Terry the photos.

"No, he's not getting sloppy," Marshall said looking back at the body. "He wasn't able to surprise her like he was the others. He had to take more risks, and that led to leaving physical evidence."

"Is there anything else you can tell us," Diana asked. "We'll wait for the official release before printing anything, but is there anything more that might help identify the killer?"

"Wait a minute," said Terry excitedly. "Does this school have a library?"

"I imagine it does," Marshall said. "But it's a school library, so I wouldn't expect much."

"Just wait," Terry said pulling out his cell phone. He punched in a phone number. Diana and Marshall could hear it ringing on the other end.

"He isn't trying to call the killer, is he?" Marshall asked.

Diana shrugged her shoulders signaling she didn't know.

"Hello, Becky? This is Terry Lambert. You know the really short guy from the bar. You were telling us the Sherlock Holmes books. Do you remember the name of the sixth book? You do. Great! What is it?" Terry wrote the title on his notebook and ended the call.

Terry faced Diana. "I just called Becky, you know, that waitress from Murphy's, the one who knows all about Sherlock Holmes."

"Okay," Diana said drawing the word out.

"She told me the name of the sixth book is *The Return of Sherlock Holmes*. I bet the killer left a clue in that book in this school's library."

"Good thinking," Marshall said. He waved to Freedman

and informed him that he and Steven were going to the school's library.

Terry was uncomfortable with the amount of noise the footsteps of five people made walking down the hall, especially with no one talking. The principal showed the group the entrance to the library. Marshall and Steven drew their weapons as a precaution. The principal made it a point to remain in the hallway, standing to one side of the doorway. Terry and Diana started to followed Marshall and Steven into the room. Marshall held up his hand and pointed to the principal indicating they should wait with him. It took Marshall and Steven a few minutes, but they were able to confirm the room was clear of any danger. Terry and Diana entered the library and located the mystery section of the library. Marshall and Steve joined them. Terry slowly pointed to a book on fifth shelf. Steven donned a pair of nitrile gloves and lifted *The Return of Sherlock Holmes* from the bookshelf. Steven found single piece of paper in the book. He read it aloud for everyone.

The dominance of pretentious individuals and their condescending attitude to the people who do the real work and are the real heart of our society can no longer be tolerated. Education is the key to awaking the power individuals have and banding them together to overthrow the corrupt corporations that buy and run our country. The greed and corruption must stop. People, the true people, deserve better treatment from our government. Power will return to those who deserve it.

"He's nuts," Terry said. "This doesn't help us at all."

"I don't think it's supposed to," Diana replied. "The message here is education is the key, and yet he kills a teacher. He says he wants greedy politicians and corporations to treat others better. It's well known that teachers are vastly underpaid. Seriously, think about it. College football coaches get paid millions of dollars while most college professors and instructors make less than six figures."

Terry sighed. "Like I said, the guy's nuts."

Marshall made sure Steven put the note in an evidence bag. While Steven was taking photographs of the where they had found the note, Marshall waved for Terry and Diana to follow him, so they would be out of Steven's way. They watched as Steven walked through the library looking for additional clues.

"I think the notes are red herrings," Marshall said. "I think they designed to lead us in the wrong direction. The notes don't make sense. There are no connections. Also, he didn't start leaving notes until the third victim. I think he doesn't want us to take too close a look at the first two victims."

"So, the notes are useless," Terry said.

"Not at all," answered Marshall. "The notes tell us he planned this murder. He carefully selected a teacher, at this school, where he knew the students wouldn't be here, but the teachers would. He probably planted this note and the book before he killed our victim. He's becoming more dangerous."

"What are you going to do?" Diana asked.

"We're going back to your friend's suggestion," Marshall answered. "We're going to focus on the first two victims and continue to look for that blue pickup truck."

~ ~ ~

He knew he would have to wait. He had seen Terry and the brunette at the school where the sixth victim was. He needed to give them time to finish up there and get back to the paper. He picked up the blood-stained shirt from his trunk. He grinned realizing the importance of hiding bloody clothing. If he hadn't, then that cop, who just doing his job, would have noticed the blood on the shirt he had worn when he stabbed that woman. He would have had to kill that cop. He wondered if killing a police officer would be as enjoyable as killing the women. Probably more so. He would have to consider murdering a cop to see what it was like. He was disappointed this time. It had been more difficult because the woman suspected something, but the killing didn't bring him the satisfaction he experienced with the others. He didn't want to kill a teacher, but he needed to kill an African-American, so the police couldn't establish a pattern. He unfolded the shirt. He noticed a small part of a sleeve was missing, along with a button. This wasn't good.

~ ~ ~

Ashford stormed into the news room. "You stole my story Runt," he screamed at Terry. "You saw me there and instead of getting me access to the scene, you went in and got the information so that you could steal the story from me."

Terry stared up at Ashford. "There are times when I really think you take stupid pills. I was there because of the phone call I got, and I was helping the police with their investigation."

"Don't give me that crap," Ashford yelled. He grabbed Terry, lifting him from his chair, and slapped Terry across his face, knock Terry to the ground.

Diana grabbed a large binder and ran up behind Ashford. She proceeded to smack him between his shoulders. "Don't you hit Terry! He's half your size. Good grief, what an ass."

Ashford began to blush. "He started it," Ashford said point to Terry, who was still on the ground.

Terry got to his feet and drew back his right leg.

"Don't you dare," Diana yelled. "Don't kick him. Ashford's an ass, and he deserves it; but don't you stoop down to his level."

169

"Everyone, knock it off," Fitch bellowed. "Ashford, Terry didn't take your story. It was his. Now you get into my office. Meanwhile, the rest of you get back to work. And Diana, quit hitting people with that notebook."

Terry brushed himself off and returned to his desk. Diana put the binder down before coming over to put her hand on Terry's shoulder. "You all right?" she asked.

"Yeah, I'm fine."

Diana pulled up a chair, sat down, and held onto Terry's arm for a moment. "No, you're not. No one likes to be bullied. You have to remember to be the adult and let it go. I know it's hard, but you can't let Ashford get to you."

Terry couldn't look Diana in the eye, but he had to. "Can you do me a favor?"

"Yeah, I know, leave you alone."

"No, it's not that," Terry said. "I was hoping you and Carl could finish up with the editing. I need to go somewhere."

"Can I ask where?"

"I wish you wouldn't."

Diana smiled. "You got it big guy."

Terry nodded thanks, grabbed his coat, and left.

~ ~ ~

It felt strange to Terry as he entered the gym. He didn't know if it was from the murder that took place a week before or because he hadn't visited a gym since he was in college. He saw Paula standing in the doorway of an exercise room, talking to three of her students. He looked around once, then a second time, before approaching Paula.

"Hey, how are you doing?" Paula said when she saw him. "What brings you here?"

Terry was aware he was the center of attention as the women looked at him, waiting for an answer.

"Excuse me ladies," Paula said to the three women. "I need to take care of something. I'll see you all next week."

"Sure thing," one of them replied.

Paula waited until they had left the gym before turning back to Terry. "Okay, what's up? Why are you here?"

"I need a favor from you." Terry answered.

"What?"

"I need you to teach me fight. I need to learn how to defend myself."

Paula crossed her arms and stared down at Terry. "What brought this on? You're a dwarf, so your opponent is always going to have the advantage. What makes you think you can take someone on, and win?"

"I just need to learn how to defend myself. You know, in case I'm attacked. I'm tired of being a victim."

"Well, in your case, I would recommend grabbing a heavy object and hitting the person in the knee. When he bends down, smack him in the head with the object in your hand. Then, hit him in the balls. If that hasn't brought down your opponent, then you're in big trouble. By the way, once your opponent is down, run away. Don't stand around, giving him a chance to recover."

"That hardly seems like a fair fight."

Paula smiled. "There is no such thing as a fair fight. When you fight, you fight to disable or kill your opponent. You don't fight because your ego is bruised. You fight because you need to overpower your opponent, or you end up getting hurt or killed. You fight for survival, not status. Now, why do you need to learn how to fight?"

"What does it matter," Terry said angrily.

Paula uncrossed her arms and got down on one knee to be face-to-face with Terry. She reached out and grabbed him by both of his shoulders. "All right, then fight. Come on. Beat me. I'm down on one knee. Come on and kick the crap out of me!"

Terry struggled to get free but couldn't. He stood there, looking down at the ground, biting his lower lip.

Paula released him and stood up. "I just defeated you,

and I didn't do anything but hold you. What's going on?"

"Ashford hit me," Terry replied quietly.

"What?"

"I said Ashford hit me," Terry repeated in a louder voice.

Paula put her hand on his shoulder. "There will always be someone bigger and stronger. Listen, being beaten, or losing a fight, is not a big deal. The way to defeat an opponent is to not let that person take control of your life. Being physically stronger is one thing. Being mentally and emotionally stronger is another. You defeat your opponent with your mind. No matter how physical he gets, as long as you don't give up, he can't win. Just remember, it's mind over matter."

"So, I just turn the other cheek and take it."

"Oh no," Paula said smiling. "I'm going to teach you how to redefine the word pain for him. No one bullies my friends and gets to walk away."

"What about the mind over matter part?"

"Well I don't mind, and he doesn't matter. Now, let's get started."

"Do I need to change into gym clothes?"

"Will you have the chance to change on the street?"

"No."

"Then you don't need to change."

Chapter Nineteen

Terry groaned as he exited the elevator the next morning. Paula had spent two hours showing him how to inflict pain on various parts of the body with everyday objects such as pens, staplers, shoes, and a water bottle with a strap. She called them *weapons of opportunity*. In addition to sore muscles, he had bruises up and down his arms and legs.

"Runt," grunted Ashford as he walked into the office.

Terry wanted to call him a jackass, but he realized it Ashford's case it would be complimentary. Fitch happened to be there when Ashford came in. He motioned for Ashford to come into his office. Terry knew he should be ashamed for feeling happy about Ashford being admonished for his bad behavior, but Terry wasn't.

"What are you grinning about?" Diana asked as she came over.

"Ashford's in trouble."

"What is it this time?"

"I think it's because he called me runt and Fitch heard it."

"So, what? All Fitch is going to do is tell him to mind his manners. There really isn't much more he can do. Ashford's a top reporter and there is no way this paper is going to fire him. By the way, how are you holding up, especially after yesterday?"

"Don't worry about me."

"Good. Anyway, I came over because I got the obituary on Daniel Kuntz. His funeral was handled by Dawson Funeral Home. I thought maybe we could stop by there later today."

"When do you want to go?"

Diana hit a few keys on her computer to bring up her calendar. "Well, I'm free after lunch. You should have most of the paper laid out by then. Why don't we go this afternoon?"

"Sounds good. Think we should call Paula?"

Diana put her hand up to her chin and took a moment before responding. "No, I don't think we need to drag her to the funeral parlor. But I'll call her and see if we can't meet up tonight. We'll fill her in then."

~ ~ ~

The morning routine at the paper now included the appearance of Stephen and a detective, who were now bringing Sherlock Holmes novels to read. The reporters were getting used to Terry running off, so they double checked their stories before submitting them. They also worked to get them in as early as possible. The result was by noon Terry had completed most of his work for the day. The only unusual aspect of the job was his sore muscles and how surprised he was at how much they ached even though he was sitting at a desk typing on a computer.

Diana came over to get Terry, who groaned as he stood up.

"Are you okay?" Diana asked.

"Yeah," Terry answered with another groan. "I worked out with Paula yesterday. I may have over did it."

"Do you think? Really, have you ever exercised? I mean, have you ever played a sport?"

"No, I didn't make the basketball team. Who would have thought it?"

"Seriously, have you ever participated in kind of organized sports or exercise program?"

Terry sheepishly looked at the ground. "I did some swimming when I was in college. But that was because of

Kristen. She liked to swim to stay in shape."

Diana put her hand on Terry's shoulder. "Then take it easy. And take my advice; don't try to keep up with a Marine."

"Enough already," Terry replied. "Let's go to the funeral home and see what we can find out about Daniel Kuntz."

~ ~ ~

Dawson Funeral Home focused on tradition. The building reminded one of colonial homesteads, with tall pillars in front of the two-story building. A chime rang when Diana and Terry entered the spacious foyer, decorated in stained cherry wood. To the left of foyer was the showroom, full of various coffins and displays of headstones and memorial plaques. The center opened to two non-denominational chapel areas, which could be converted into one room if necessary. To the right was a hallway leading to several business offices. A middle-aged, bald man in a dark suit emerged from one of the offices.

"Good afternoon. I'm David McDermitt. How may I be of service to you?"

"Good afternoon. I'm Diana Hawley and this is Terry Lambert. We work for *City Times* and were hoping you could tell us about the services you offer here."

"I'd be glad to, but I must tell you that we can't afford any kind of advertising at this time."

"Oh no, we're not selling advertising. We're doing research about funeral homes and the services they provide."

McDermitt raised his eyebrows. "Seriously my dear. Everyone knows what services we provide. We arrange for loved ones' final journey here on earth. The only real difference between funeral homes is mostly the price they charge; and I can assure you our prices are quite reasonable."

Diana smiled back at McDermitt. "No, we are more

interested in what kind of music, whether it is taped or if there is a live organist; the flower arrangements; the guest registry; military honors, etc."

"Now I understand," McDermitt replied inviting Diana and Terry to follow him to his office. "Please take a seat," he said as he brought out a large leather covered binder. "If you take a look here, you can see some of the special services we can offer."

Terry opened the binder. He and Diana took their time looking at each page before turning it. "You know," Terry said while turning a page, "a problem I would have is knowing who attended the funeral. Do you have people register when they attend funerals here?"

"That is up to the family?" McDermitt answered. "If they wish, we do provide a guest registry for them."

"Is it a book?" Terry asked.

"Yes, it is," McDermitt replied as he brought out a sample for Terry to see.

"I always have a problem with those," Terry said looking at the guest registry. "So many people have such terrible handwriting."

"I know what you mean. But there is very little we can do about that."

"I've heard some funeral homes are going to computer sign in," Diana added.

"We thought about that, but customers are so concern about their privacy, we felt it was better to continue with a traditional guest registry."

"What if you can't read the person's handwriting?" Diana asked.

"Well with the address, phone number, and email address; hopefully you would be able to realize who the person was; or at least contact that individual."

"Do you keep copies of the guest registries?" Terry asked.

"No, we don't. We release the registry to the family after the funeral."

"You know, a friend of ours recommended your place," Terry said as he continued to look through the binder. "They said you did a great job with a funeral of someone they knew, Daniel Kuntz. Do you think you could give us the family's address so that we can contact them for a reference?"

"No," McDermitt strongly stated. "We take privacy very seriously here. And I am beginning to suspect you are not here to examine our services."

"Why do you say that?" Terry asked.

McDermitt grinned. "If a friend of yours had recommended us, you would not need that person's address. So, what do you really need?"

"I'm sure you've read about the Sherlock Holmes Murders," Diana answered. "There is a possibility that Kuntz family may be able to help us identify the killer. I can't go into detail; but I can assure you it is very important that we talk to the family."

MCDermitt took a moment before replying. "I'm sorry, but there is nothing that I can do. I must protect the privacy of our clients."

Diana held up a hand to signal understanding. "How about you help us out here. I'll give you my card, and you can call the family and ask them to contact us. That way, their privacy is maintained, and we get the information we need."

"What information do you need?"

Diana held out one of her business cards. "We just need to ask the family a few questions about who attended the funeral. A few questions and that's all. Can you just call them and ask them to meet us?"

"Yes, I can do that." McDermitt said taking Diana's card.

~ ~ ~

"Howdy friends," Becky said as she set down drinks in front of Paula, Terry, and Diana. "I love it when regulars keep coming back to Murphy's. It's kind of like that song they used to have for that TV show *Cheers*, everybody knows your name."

"Thank you," Diana said as she picked up her drink.

Paula grinned as she picked up hers. "What I like is I don't need to order. You already know what I want."

Becky put her hand on Terry shoulder. He flinched. "How are you doing?"

"He's a bit sore," Paula answered. "He started working out with me and I may have been a bit too rough with him."

"Ah," Becky said gently rubbing Terry's shoulder. "Do you want some ibuprofen?"

Terry patted Becky's hand. "Nah, I'll be okay."

Paula took a sip from her drink. "Tell you what I suggest, you should exercise some when you get home. Nothing strenuous, just some simple stretches and maybe a few pushups. The exercise will help the soreness go away quicker."

Becky, in her usual perky mood, clapped her hands together. "Hey, if you really want to get in shape, you all can join me for jazz dance. There is a class at the university and it's really cheap, and a lot of fun."

Terry got out of his chair, placed his hands on his hips, and started kicking. "Yeah, I can see me at jazz dancing. One, two, three, kick."

Diana and Paula giggled.

"Actually, it's not a bad idea," Paula said. "Dancing is great exercise and it would give you confidence."

Terry sat back down. "I'd rather continue with the training we started, if you don't mind?"

"No problem," was Paula's reply.

Becky picked up her tray from the table. "Well, if you guys are all set, I'll get back to my other customers."

Paula laid a ten-dollar bill on the tray. "Becky, thank you. Appreciate your consideration. Seriously, thank you."

Becky smiled and waved as she walked away.

Diana leaned forward. "Guess what?"

"What?" Paula answered. "Did I get it right?"

Diana stared at Paula, confused.

"You said 'guess what,' and I guessed 'what.' Hey, it was a joke," Paula said responding to Diana's disapproving look.

"Anyway," Diana replied with a slight wave of her hand. "Terry and I went to the funeral home today. The one where Daniel Kuntz had his services. They don't have computer registries, but the funeral director said he would contact Daniel Kuntz's family and see if they would let us talk to them."

"Good work," Paula said, taking a sip of her drink. "Anything else?"

"No, nothing. Anything on your end?" Terry asked.

"No, I spent the day teaching exercise classes. There were a lot of people leaving flowers and cards for Kelly. When I got finished, I took everything over to her family who are staying in a hotel. They asked me to help them with cleaning out Kelly's apartment. I'll go over and do that tomorrow."

Terry put down his mug of beer. "Boy, today has been a big disappointment. We haven't made any progress on the case."

"Hi, I'm back," Becky said as she pulled out a chair and sat down.

"Don't you have other customers?" Paula asked.

"Of course, I do," Becky replied. "But I wanted to ask about your friend."

"What about her," Paula responded with a degree of irritation.

"Well, I read in the newspaper. It was your newspaper by the way," Becky said motioning to Diana and Terry.

"That your friend was a victim of this serial killer the call the 'Sherlock Holmes Killer.' Now I don't know much about crime solving, except for what I see on TV. But don't serial killers usually take some kind of trophy; something from the victim, so that they can remember the crime, kind of relive it or something?"

"She's right," Diana replied. "I've ready that too. Serial killers do often take some kind of trophy."

Terry grabbed his backpack and pulled out the autopsy files. I have the files here, maybe we can find out what the killer took."

"Oh, how terrible," Becky said when she saw the crime scene photos. "I don't want to look at those. I was just suggesting that if you could figure out what the killer takes from the victims, it might give you a clue."

"How are we going to do that?" Terry asked

"Personal effects," Paula answered. "Let's look at their personal effects and see if we can find anything missing."

Terry went through the files and pulled out the lists of each victim's personal effects. Everyone at the table spent several minutes carefully reading each file."

"I give up," Terry said. "I have no idea of what to look for."

"It's true," Diana agreed. "If there is a clue here, I don't see it."

"Well, I don't know if it's a clue or not," Becky said unsure of herself, "but none of them have any earrings. I mean it's not unusual for one woman not to have earrings, and I guess if two of them didn't, it could be a coincidence. But for all of these women, and not one of them have earrings."

Paula smiled and gave Becky a pat on her shoulder.

"What? I did it," Becky said with surprise. "I found a clue. It's earrings?"

~ ~ ~

The memorial was still at the entrance to Walmart when Paula, Terry, and Diana came in. A silver-haired woman with the blue Walmart vest was seated on a stool. She smiled as the trio walked in. "Good evening. What can we do for you tonight?" she asked.

Diana returned the smile. "I'm hoping we could talk to Joseph Simms. Is he working tonight?"

"Joseph! Why he's a sweetheart of a boy," the greeter answered. "I don't know if he is working or not; but if he's here, he would be in the electronic section. That's at the back of the store."

Diana squeezed the greeter's hand. "Thank you. We'll just go back and see if he's there."

The three of them walked to the back of the store, where they found Joseph behind a cash register. This time Paula was the spokesperson. "Hey, Joseph. Need to talk to you."

"Certainly," the young man replied. "What can I do for you?"

"Do you remember us? We were here a few days ago asking about your friend, Frances Colton."

"Of course, I recognized you."

"It may sound a bit odd, but do you know if Frances wore earrings?"

"Woah! That's a strange one. Of course, she wore earrings."

"How do you know?" Paula asked.

"Well, I remember we had a big sale on them in the jewelry department. She got her boyfriend to buy her a set of diamond ones. She wore those all the time."

"Wait," Diana interjected. "Her boyfriend bought her diamond earrings?"

"Yep," Joseph said nodding his head.

"Is there anything else you can tell us about her boyfriend?" Terry pleaded.

"Not really," Joseph said turning his head in an effort to

remember some detail for the three standing in front of him. "I think he graduated college because I remember Frances used her employee discount to get him some kind of computer software. I think it was a graduation gift, but I can't be sure. I mean I never met the guy, so I really don't know. I know he was making good money. He bought Frances those earrings. Even with the employee discount and with them being on sale, they still cost quite a bit."

"Any idea about what he did? What kind of job he had?" Paula asked.

Joseph shook his head. "No, not really. Must have been some kind of computer job because I know he worked from home."

Chapter Twenty

Terry noticed Ashford was already in the office when he arrived the next morning. Terry felt anxiety creep into his soul, waiting for an attack from his office nemesis. Terry kept his eyes focused on Ashford as he walked to his desk. Ashford continued to look at his computer screen. Terry pulled out his chair and checked it to be sure there wasn't anything wrong. He sat down and turned on his computer. Then he saw it.

"How dare you," Terry yelled grabbing the picture of his wife. There was a moustache drawn in black ink on the photograph. "You ruined it." Terry threw the photo at Ashford.

"What's your problem?" Ashford said acting surprised.

Terry ran toward Ashford just as Fitch walked in. Terry grabbed a coffee mug, the nearest object on Ashford's desk. He swung it back, ready to strike Ashford.

Fitch reached out and grabbed Terry's arm. "What are you doing?" Fitch demanded. "Why are you attacking Ashford?"

"Really," Ashford added. "All I was doing was sitting here when all of a sudden, he goes crazy."

Terry picked up Kristen's picture from the floor. "Look at what he did. He drew a moustache on her. A picture of my wife. My personal property. And he ruined it."

"Hey, it could have been anybody," Ashford said holding up his arms. "I'm innocent. Who said I did it."

"I know it was you," Terry yelled, looking for another object for another attack.

Fitch pulled Terry away. "Hey, go back to your desk. I understand you're upset about someone defacing the picture of your dead wife. But let me handle this. I can't have you attacking people. Now just go back and try to calm down."

"Calm down. I'll calm down when I kick his ass."

Ashford giggled. "Really, a runt like you is going to kick my ass."

"Ashford, shut up," Fitch bellowed. "You're not helping the situation."

Terry threw his arms down to his sides, continuing to stare at Ashford. "You're lucky this time, but your time is running out. I'm not going to let this go."

"Sounds like a threat," Ashford stated.

"No, it's a promise," Terry answered before turning and returning to his desk.

Fitch signaled for Ashford to follow him to the editor's office. Others were entering the office and Fitch did not want to deal with the situation in front of the staff. One of the reporters noticed the broken glass from the picture and got a broom and dustpan to clean it up.

Terry carefully took the photograph from the broken frame. He threw the broken frame in the trash and place the photo in a desk drawer. He glared at his computer screen. He took several deep breaths, hoping to calm down enough to where he could work. His meditation was interrupted by the ringing of his phone. He started to reach for it. His hand was less than a foot away. Terry turned to see the recording machine, but Stephen hadn't come in yet. The phone rang a second time. Terry ran over and turned on the machine before picking up the receiver.

"Good morning Terry." It was the voice. "Did you miss me?"

"Knock off the crap," Terry yelled into the phone. "You're a sick son of a bitch who hurts innocent people. Do the world a favor and step in front of a bus."

"Hey," the voice yelled back. "You don't get to talk to me that way. If you don't want me to call, fine. I'll call some other newspaper."

"No you won't," Terry answered vehemently. "You love the attention we're giving you. If you were to start calling someone else, they wouldn't believe you. They would think you're some kind of kook, trying to get false publicity. No, you're stuck with me. Now, tell me about the poor girl you killed you sicko."

"Kiss off," the voice said before hanging up.

Terry slammed down the phone. *Crap*, he thought, *I really blew it this time. We'll never find the body of his latest victim.* The phone rang again. Terry hesitatingly picked up the receiver.

"*City Times*, copy editing," Terry said as he put the receiver to his ear.

"Terry, this is Detective Marshall. We have another body. I think our friend has struck again. Has he called this morning?"

Terry closed his eyes and leaned back in his chair. He opened his eyes. "Yeah, he called. It was just a few minutes ago. Luckily Steven showed me how to turn on the recording machine, so I was able to record his call. Unfortunately, I lost my temper with him and he hung up before telling me anything. Sorry."

"Don't be," Marshall replied. "I'll have Stephen check out the recording later. Right now, I'd like for you to come down Meadow Lark Apartments on Kingston Avenue. I'm sure you'll find us once you get here."

Terry hung up the phone and turned off the machine. He was heading out when he ran into Diana.

"Where are you going?" she asked.

"Detective Marshall just called. There's another murder victim. Do you want to come along?"

"Absolutely," Diana answered as she followed Terry out the door.

~ ~ ~

This is great, he thought. No one suspected who he was. As far as anyone was concerned, he was a resident relaxing by the pool. He had stolen the girl's pool pass along with her keys. Now he had a front-row seat while the police did their thing. Even though there were several others gathered around to see the action, they were all close to the yellow crime scene tape. He was so far in the background, no one would notice him. Still, he kept sunglasses on to help disguise him from the residents and Terry.

Terry had upset him when he called. He thought about calling again, even though the police were already on the scene. To his delight, a car soon appeared, and he saw Terry and the pretty brunette get out. It turns out he wouldn't need to call again.

~ ~ ~

Meadow Lark Apartments were a series of four-unit buildings stretched out in a U-shaped pattern with a large parking lot in the middle. Behind the apartments were an open field on one side, a trailer park on the other, and a wooden lot. It was the wooden lot where the body laid.

"What happened," Terry asked when he and Diana arrived.

Freedman waved them over. "The victim is a 27-year-old female, Asian-American, named Naomi Yamato. She was stabbed twice in the back. She's a payroll clerk at a factory. She lives in the apartment complex. Her keys were missing, so we think the killer took the keys and went into her apartment. Stephen has already gone into her apartment, where he found a Sherlock Holmes novel, *The Valley of Fear*. There was a note in it, same kind of crap our killer has been spewing."

"But it's different this time," Diana stated. "He picked an

Asian woman and he didn't call leaving us a clue where to find the body."

"Yes, he did," Terry interjected. "He called, but I got angry and he hung up."

"We found the body anyway," Freedman added. "But that was just luck. A jogger was running by and saw it."

"Good thing or we would have never found it," Diana said.

"Not true," Terry replied. "Each body was publicly displayed. Each victim was some place where someone would have found them; it was only a matter of time. The killer's clues just ensured we found them in time to make the news. This guy is more concerned with getting publicity than anything else."

"But there is no pattern," Diana pointed out.

"That's right," agreed Terry. "But remember what Becky said. What if this guy is doing this on purpose, to screw up any kind of forensics or profiling?"

"Who's Becky?" Freedman asked.

"Oh, there's this waitress we know who had this idea," Diana began explaining. "She thought maybe the killer had a job like being a book agent or editor, someone who would have access to lots of mystery novels and police stories. That person would know how to avoid the detection and how to leave false clues. We know he wants publicity more than anything else, so the victims are just random and there is no pattern to follow. This makes it harder to catch him."

"Why does this waitress think he's a mystery novel buff and not someone studying criminal justice or a former police officer?"

"It's the Sherlock Holmes novels," Terry answered. "Only someone with a literary interest would use a different Sherlock Holmes novel with each victim. Also, the novels correspond to the victims. For example, this is the seventh victim, and I bet the novel, *The Valley of Fear*, is the seventh Sherlock Holmes novel."

Freedman smiled. "Turns out there is a pattern after all."

"We may also have another lead," Terry added. "We know the killer used the name of Daniel Kuntz, a person who died several months ago. We went to the funeral home that handled his burial. We are hoping to get the address of his family and a look at the guest registry. Hopefully, that will give us the killer's real name."

Freedman took out his notebook again. "What's the name of the funeral home?"

"Dawson Funeral Home and the name he used was Daniel Kuntz," Terry replied proudly. "And we found another clue."

Freedman stood there with his pen poised over his notebook. "You going to tell me, or am I going to have read about it in the papers?"

"Of course," Terry exclaimed. "We went through the autopsy reports and discovered that none of the victims had earrings. We think the killer takes the victims' earrings as a kind of trophy. Serial killers do that you know."

Freedman chuckled. "Yeah, we know. We also noticed the absence of earrings from the victims' effects. We like to keep one or two details from the public. It helps us make sure we have the right guy when we pick up a suspect."

"You already knew about it?" Diana asked.

"Yeah, we knew," Freedman answered. "Give us a break, will you? We're detectives. We've been doing this for quite a while."

~ ~ ~

The elevator dinged, signaling his floor. Terry pushed off the back of the elevator where he had been leaning. "Yea, we're back,"

Diana held the button on the elevator for them to get off. "Yea, more fun."

"Where have you two been," Fitch demanded. "Work here started five hours ago."

"Please, give us a break," Diana pleaded. "We have just spent the last four hours at a crime scene."

"Is it that mysterious caller?" an excited Fitch asked.

"Yeah, it's that demented individual," Terry answered. "He killed another poor girl."

"Woman," Diana corrected. "The victim was a young woman, not a girl."

"Sorry for not being politically correct," Terry replied.

Fitch waved his head toward the copy desk. "You got the story? Right? Write it up."

Terry stood in the middle of the room. "I'm not in the mood."

"What is this crap about being in *the mood*?" Fitch demanded. "This is a newspaper. Reporters write stories whether they are in the mood or not."

Diana put her hands on Terry's shoulders and steered him to his desk. "Fitch is right. It's news and we've got to print it. She deserves it."

"No, she doesn't deserve to become news by being a victim. Nobody does. She should make headlines for her great accomplishments in business or helping others in the community, not for being murdered. I'm sure the last thing her family wants is to see her name in print as a murder victim."

"You're right about that," Diana said over her shoulder as she returned to her desk. She sat down and noticed the blinking red light on her phone signaling she had voice mail.

Diana pushed the button. She listened to the message. "Terry," she exclaimed with excitement, "I got a message from Daniel Kuntz's widow. She's willing to meet with us."

Terry sat quietly for a moment before answering. "Great. You set up an appointment. I'll write the story about the woman at Meadow Lark. See if we can get Paula to come along."

"Why?"

"Do you know what we are looking for?" Terry asked.

Diana gave him a half smile. "You're right, I don't. I hope Paula does."

~ ~ ~

The Kuntz home was a modest townhouse with two large pine trees in the front yard. Diana rang the doorbell, which was immediately answer with the barking of two large dogs on the other side of the door.

"I hope they're friendly," Terry said stepping back from the door.

"If not, we'll feed them you first," Paula joked.

An elderly woman opened the door, turned to the two golden retrievers behind her, and barked out the command to sit. Both dogs immediately did.

"They're well trained," Diana commented.

"Yes, they are," answered the elderly woman. "My late husband trained military working dogs when he was in the service. Now, how can I help you?"

"I'm Diana Hawley. I called you on the phone about your husband's funeral. This is Terry Lambert. He works with me. And this is my friend Paula Stanford."

"Oh yes, I remember your friend from when she was here the first time. Please come in," the elderly woman said opening the screen door. As soon as everyone entered, the dogs got up and ran over with their tails wagging. "Oh, don't mind them. They just want to play. They'll lick you to death, but they won't hurt you."

Paula reached down and ruffled the fur of each one. "That's okay. I love dogs."

The woman led everyone into the living room furnished with a large cloth covered sofa and two chairs. Two large cloth cushions for the dogs were against the wall. "Well, come on in and make yourselves comfortable. Can I get you some coffee or tea?"

"That's very kind of you," Diana answered. "But I'm kind of hoping we won't take up too much of your time."

"That's okay. I don't get many visitors, so what company does come to the door, I enjoy."

Diana smiled as everyone took a seat. She realized she had become the de facto spokesperson. "First of all, let us express our condolences on the passing of your husband. May I ask how he passed?"

"Why thank you dear. He had cancer. After smoking those smelly cigars for all those years, it's no surprise. I miss him, but I'm glad his suffering is over."

Diana placed her hand on Mrs. Kuntz's. "I understand. I hate to bother you with details, but I was hoping you could show us the guest registry from your husband's funeral."

"Why sure dear, but what for?" Mrs. Kuntz said as she got up and walked over to drawer located under the television. "Here you are," she said handing it to Diana.

Diana handed the registry to Paula, who started looking through it.

"What are you looking for?" asked Mrs. Kuntz.

"May I ask what your husband did for a living?" asked Paula.

"He was a contractor. Home remolding and such."

"Did he own a truck?"

"No, but he did have a van. After Daniel died, Billy bought it from me."

"Who is Billy?" Terry asked.

"He's a young man that helped Daniel at times," Mrs. Kuntz replied.

Paula leaned over to Mrs. Kuntz. "Could you point out Billy's name and address for us? We might be able to use his help with a project we are working on."

"Of course, dear," Mrs. Kuntz said pointing to a name in the middle of the page. "That's him. If you want, I could call him for you."

"Oh no, that's not necessary," Paula answered waving her hand. "We have to check a few things out first before we can call anyone."

"I understand dear. But Billy isn't really in the construction business. Before he went to college, he worked with Daniel on quite a few jobs. But after college, he took a new job."

Paula smiled and showed Diana an entry in the registry. Next to Billy's name was another guest's name – Frances Colton, the first victim found behind the abandon shopping center.

"I hate to be nosy and I realize it's personal," Terry said clearing his throat. "How old was your husband when he passed?"

"Oh, he wasn't that old. He wasn't a spring chicken; but at sixty-five he could still carry a fifty-pound sack on his shoulders. But he was getting up there in years. That's why he would ask Billy to help him."

"How old is Billy?" Terry asked.

"Why he's a young man. He just turned thirty-two a few months ago."

Paula handed the guest registry back to Mrs. Kuntz. "Excuse me, but you said Billy had a new job. What kind of job allowed him to take time off to help your husband?

"Oh, he's one of those fancy free-lance book editors. He gets to work from home, doesn't need to go into an office. Everything is done through computers nowadays."

Terry grunted in an effort to push aside one of the large dogs between him and Mrs. Kuntz. "Did Billy own a pickup truck?"

"Why yes he did."

"What color is his truck?" Terry continued to push against the dog which wasn't moving. It seemed to enjoy the contest.

"If I remember correctly, it's blue."

Chapter Twenty-One

"**W**e've got him," Terry said excitedly as he, Diana, and Paula got into Paula's car. "We have his name, we know he drives a blue pickup, he knew Daniel Kuntz; we got him."

Paula put the keys in the ignition. "No, we don't."

"What?!"

"We have a man who drives a blue pickup and knew Daniel Kuntz, which we suspect he used as an alias. However, we have no proof tying him to any crime."

"So, what do we do?" Terry asked.

"We get proof," Paula answered as she put her car in gear. "First we go to the police and tell them what we found out."

"And after that?"

"We'll let the police decide."

~ ~ ~

Terry glanced at his watch and noted they had been waiting in the police station for almost an hour. He looked over at Paula and wondered how she could be so relaxed. Again, he was swinging his feet back and forth, which dangled from the chair where he was sitting. Meanwhile, Paula was leaned back against the wall with her feet stretched out in front of her. She had her eyes closed. Terry wondered if she was asleep or not.

"Will you settle down," Diana said as she looked at her smart phone again.

"Why?" Terry replied. "Either you are waiting for a very important phone call or you're as bored as I am."

"What makes you say that?"

Terry pointed to her cell phone. "You've checked that thing every two minutes since we got here."

"Yeah, well police stations don't come with waiting rooms," Paula said with her eyes still closed. It answered one question, she wasn't asleep.

Detective Marshall walked up. Paula sat up and pulled her feet in. "We ran the name you gave us," Marshall said looking at a piece of paper in his hand. "The person's name is William James Dunn, aka Billy. He's thirty-two and self-employed as a book editor. He does own a blue pickup. We're going to his address, and I would like you all to come along. Maybe you can identify him as the person you saw at the fairgrounds the night Emily Kemper was murdered."

"Of course," Diana answered. "But even if we do recognize him, all I can say is he was there at the fairgrounds that night."

"And, I didn't see anyone that night," Paula replied.

"No, but maybe you can recognize the truck that tried to run you off the road."

"That's easy. Just look for a bullet hole in the tailgate. I may have missed the driver, but I didn't miss the truck."

Marshall gave Paula a small smile. "Still, why don't you come along anyway?"

"Yes," Terry shouted jumping off of the chair. "Let's go and arrest that son of a bitch."

"Whoa, you're a real militant midget, aren't you?" Paula said standing up.

"I'm not a midget. I'm a dwarf."

Paula patted Terry on the shoulder. "Sorry."

~ ~ ~

Ashford turned off the portable police scanner as he pulled up behind one of the three unmarked police sedans parked on the street in front of single-story house with a double garage. He hadn't seen any patrol units, but he was sure they were close by.

"What is the press doing here?" Freedman demanded when he saw Ashford approaching.

"*Freedom of the Press* brother," Ashford shouted back. "I have every right to cover this story, and you can't stop me."

Marshall and several of the other detectives stared at Ashford.

"What story?" Freedman asked.

"Hah, hah," Ashford said with a fake laugh. "The Sherlock Holmes Murders of course. I know you have a suspect and you're about to make an arrest."

"No," Freedman replied, "we have a person of interest."

"Hey, you don't have to explain anything to him," Marshall stated.

"Well, I'm here in case you do make an arrest."

Terry looked up and the sky and slapped his hands against his legs before looking at Ashford. "Good grief, you're such an asshole."

Ashford came over and confronted Terry. "Watch it Runt. And stay away from my story."

"It's my story," Terry vehemently responded.

Ashford raised his hand and back slapped Terry across the face. "Stay away runt!"

Freedman grabbed Ashford's arm and spun him around, throwing him onto the hood of the nearest car. "Thanks idiot. You just committed an assault, and now you're under arrest."

"You can't arrest me. I'm a member of the press." Ashford screamed.

Freedman put handcuffs on Ashford and thrust him to another detective. "Take him in." Freedman leaned over to the detective and whispered in his ear. "Make sure to take your time. It wouldn't upset anyone if he had to spend the night in lock up."

Marshall waved his hand to gather the others around him. "Enough of this commotion. We're attracting too much attention already." He pointed to two detectives and sent them around the back of the house. Everyone else, including Paula, Diana, and Terry, followed Marshall to the front door. He made sure everyone was standing to the side and not in front of the door. He knocked on the door and wait.

~ ~ ~

Who are they? What are they doing in front of my house?

He smiled. It was a good thing he had to run to the hardware store to get some supplies. He was almost home before he saw the cars parked in front of his house. He drove his van past the cars and the people, who he was sure were cops, and pulled to the curb three houses down the block.

In his rear-view mirrors, he could see a man, who claim he was a reporter. The man in the van realized the police and the press knew who he was. Billy's anger tempered when he saw the tall blond woman and Terry get out of an unmarked sedan. He was even happier when he saw the pretty brunette get out too. Billy watched as a man claimed he was a reporter and began to shout, then hit Terry. He had to suppress a laugh at Terry being hit and the reporter's struggle against being arrested. The police, Terry, the pretty brunette, and the tall blond went up to his front door and knocked. *How did that half-sized man find me?* Billy realized he needed to leave before the police started checking cars on the street. He started the engine and pulled the van away from the curb. The police were still waiting for someone to answer the door.

~ ~ ~

Marshall knocked on the door a second time. Still no answer. Paula left the group standing at the door and moved to the garage. She bent down to grab to the handle of the garage door.

"Don't," Marshall shouted. "We need a warrant before we can open any door. For now, we have to limit ourselves to looking through the windows."

"You know we'll find the pickup that ran me off the road in there," Paula said pointing at the garage.

Freedman and two of the detectives began walking around the house, looking in windows, hoping to find a reason to enter the home. A few minutes later, they returned with the two detectives that had been covering the back of the house.

"Nothing," Freedman said, holstering his pistol. "It doesn't look like any one is home. We looked in a window to the garage. There was a vehicle in there, but it was covered with a large plastic tarp. It looked like it could be a pickup, but I couldn't tell for sure from the window."

Marshall pointed to two of the detectives. "You two, start a canvas of the neighbors. See if you can find out anything that might be useful. After that, stake out the place. I'll be back as soon as I get a warrant. If our suspect does return, call me before doing anything."

"You got it," answered one of the detectives giving Marshall a thumbs up sign.

~ ~ ~

"Come here Runt!" screamed Ashford as Terry walked into the editorial office. Ashford came up to Terry and shoved him back against a wall. He stood over Terry, jabbing a finger into his chest. "You got me arrested Runt!"

"You got yourself arrested," Terry replied. "You're the one who hit me. You're the one interfering with a police investigation."

"Don't give me that," Ashford continued to scream. "This is my story, and you are interfering with that investigation."

"Hey," Terry interrupted, "how did you get out? You

should still be jail. They arrested you less than an hour ago."

"It's called having a good lawyer. And you had better not press charges either, you wimp. Someone slaps you and you go crying to the police."

"You did it in front of them, you moron. I didn't do anything. It's all you."

"Enough," Fitch bellowed. He walked up to Ashford and forced him to move away from Terry. "I don't care what happened out there. Don't bring it to the office. Seriously, you're both adults. Act like it."

"Then keep that runt away from my story."

"Actually, it's *my story*," Terry replied. "It's always been my story. I'm the one that nutcase calls. I'm the one who has been at every crime scene. I'm the one working with the police. You're just the one who wants the byline because it's getting more attention than anything you are working on. So! Stay away from *my story*!"

Ashford pushed he way around Fitch and shoved Terry. He raised his hand to strike Terry. Terry put up his arm to protect himself. A hand reached out and grabbed Ashford's arm.

"Pick on someone your own size."

Ashford turned to see whose hand held his arm. He pulled, trying to free his arm, but a huge black fist held tight. Attached to the fist was a large black man wearing a hat identifying him as a taxi driver. Woody Dumfries was not going to let go.

"Who are you?" Ashford demanded.

Woody released Ashford's arm. "I'm the person telling you not to bully anyone who is smaller than you. If you want to fight someone, then I'm available."

"I take it he's your friend," Ashford said pointing to Woody with his thumb.

"That's right, I'm his friend," Woody answered. "You got a problem with that?"

"Never mind. Later Runt." Ashford walked away, staring at Woody.

"Who are you and what are you doing here?" Fitch asked

Woody waved his hand towards Terry. "I need to talk to this guy. Didn't think it would be a problem."

"Well, this is a newspaper office, and we do have a problem with people walking in off the street demanding to see employees," Fitch replied trying to act confident as he confronted the large individual. "How do I know you're not some nut case here to shoot up the place?"

"You don't," Woody answered.

"So why are you're here?" Fitch asked, sounding less confident.

"I'm here because of my sister. She was murdered."

"Wait," Ashford shouted. "Someone killed your sister. Who? What happened?"

Woody pointed his finger at Ashford. "You don't get to ask. I don't deal with bullies. Besides, I came to talk to the little guy."

"Me?" Terry asked with surprise. "Why? And what do I have to do with your sister?"

"You remember me?"

"Of course," Terry answered. "You're the taxi driver that took me to the shopping center where we found the first murder victim."

"That's right."

"So why do you need to see me?"

"Like I said, my sister was murdered."

A look of astonishment overtook Terry. "That was your sister who was killed at the school."

"That's right. And I read the paper, so I know you are helping the police find the killer. Well, I want to help too."

Terry held up his hands to calm the big man. "I can appreciate that, really. But, I'm just the guy who answers the phone. The police are the ones handling the case."

Woody sighed and looked down at the floor.

"But I do have some good news though," Terry said.

Before he could continue, Terry's phone rang.

Everyone stopped.

Terry looked around and saw everyone watching him, waiting for him to answer the phone. It rang again.

Terry hesitantly approached his desk. He stared at the phone. It rang for the third time.

Terry picked it up. "*City Times,* copy editing. Can I help you?"

"Hello Terry," the voice said.

Anger covered Terry's face. "Hello Billy. What do you want?"

"All right," the voice yelled. "So, you know who I am. But I knew that because I saw you at my house earlier. Well, the game's not over yet. I'll be in touch Terry. Just wanted to let you know that I'm not quite done yet." The voice hung up.

"It was him, wasn't it," Fitch exclaimed. "Where is the body this time?"

"There isn't one," Terry answered. "He just wanted to warn me."

"You know who the killer is," Woody bellowed. "You knew, and you still let him go. Now my sister's dead because of you wanted to sell newspapers."

"No," Terry shouted back. "We found out who he was and notified the police immediately. We've been working with them along trying to catch the guy. Honestly, getting this guy off the streets is, and always has been, our number one interest."

"Really?" Woody said scowling.

Diana came up and put her hand on Woody's arm. "Absolutely. Everyone here is working to catch this guy. We report the news; but we do care about the people who are affected by it. No one here would ever do anything to harm someone."

"So, you know who the guy is," Woody stated, "Then let's go and get the son of a bitch."

"The police are on it," Terry replied. "They have his house staked out and it's only a matter of time before they catch him."

"So, then what does the phone call mean?" Fitch asked.

Terry faced Fitch. "It means he's now making this personal."

~ ~ ~

Billy banged the phone down. He didn't know why he was angry. So the police knew his name and where he lived. He knew that. He had seen them at his house earlier in the day. He wasn't sure what to do. He silently cursed himself. He shouldn't have called Terry. He shouldn't have given Terry any warning. Then he smiled. He had a new plan.

Billy drove back to his neighborhood, parking far enough away not to attract the attention of the police staked out in front of his house. It didn't take him long to find someone to help him. He gave the kid twenty dollars, and hid behind a large SUV, a place where he could watch without being seen. He snickered as the kid approach the cop car. He couldn't hear what the kid was saying, but by the kid's gestures, he was sure the kid was telling the cops exactly what he wanted them to hear. The cops thanked the kid before leaving. The kid returned to where he was hiding, for another twenty-dollar bill. Billy paid the kid and waited for him to leave before walking up to his garage. He opened the door, pulled the plastic tarp off of his pickup. It still had the badly damaged side and the bullet hole in the tailgate. He knew it was a risk to drive it, but it would be dark in an hour and that would help him from being spotted. But after tonight, no one would ever find the truck. He needed it for one last job. He back the truck out of the garage, got out and closed the garage door. He hoped when the police returned, they wouldn't look in the garage and wouldn't know he had taken the truck.

Billy drove off. Terry and that tall blond had wanted to find this truck. Well, tonight they would.

Chapter Twenty-Two

Pretty good gym, Woody thought as he followed Terry into the building. "So, what are we doing here?" he asked.

"It's that phone call," Terry answered. "It's got me worried so I'm hoping my friend here can teach me a few moves to defend myself.

"What is he going to teach you? Karate? Judo?"

"She," Paula stated loudly to correct Woody, "is going to teach him street fighting. Is that all right with you?"

"Sure," Woody replied shrugging his shoulders. "You don't mind if I watch, do you?"

"Not at all. Back for another lesson," she said nodding to Terry, "and I see you brought someone with you."

"I'm Woody Dumfries," Woody said as he extended his hand.

Paula took his hand and shook it. "Paula Stanford." She turned to Terry. "So, what do you want to do today?"

"The killer called me just before I came over here. I was hoping you could show me a few more moves, things I could do to defend myself.

Paula led the three of them into an empty exercise room. She motioned for Terry to come at her. He did, and she quickly spun him around and pinned Terry's shoulders to a wall. "Fight me," she demanded.

Terry struggled, trying to get loose from Paula's grip.

"Fight me!"

"I'm trying," Terry said as he continued to struggle. He started to kick; but stopped short of actually making contact with Paula's legs.

"Hey, give him a break," Woody yelled. "He's a little guy. You're a lot bigger than him."

"Quiet," Paula demanded. "He's going to have to learn to fight back, and fight against everyone who is bigger than him. That's it. Keep kicking. Don't be afraid of hurting someone."

Terry screamed and kicked Paula in the shins. She still held him to the wall. Terry screamed louder and kicked harder, this time kicking her in the thigh. Her grip slackened. Terry screamed again, started to flay his arms wildly, hitting Paula's forearms.

"Yes. That's it. Fight."

With renewed energy, Terry flayed his arms and managed to grab Paula's arm. He pulled. She released him. Terry stood there, breathing heavily.

Paula looked at the red marks on her arm. She knew there would be bruises there the next day, but she didn't care. "How do you feel?" she asked.

"Pissed."

"Good! That's how you win. You get angry. You fight back. You do anything you can. You hit, you kick, you bite, you scream, you fight.

"What about people who are bigger than him?" Woody asked. "This guy at the office pushed him around because he was bigger than Terry."

"No, you let him," Paula said pointing at Terry. "Your size doesn't matter. If you let others bully you, then they will. But if you stand up to them; win, lose, tie, or draw; they quit bullying you. Their greatest weapon is you believing they can get away with it. When they learn you will fight, they back down. Remember, most bullies are cowards. They will run from a fight."

"But the person I'm most afraid of isn't a bully," Terry added.

"I know. It's the killer" Paula stated. Paula picked a towel and wiped the sweat from her face. "What did he say to you?"

"He said the game isn't over. He's pissed because we know who he is and where he lives."

Paula smiled. "He's toying with you. He's scared. The police are closing in and he wants to win this game. The only way he can do it is by hurting you. And he is doing exactly what an enemy wants to do—he wants to scare you. If he can scare you, then he has the advantage. Many times, it isn't the strongest physically who win; it is the one who is stronger mentally."

"But he's bigger than me."

"I know. You're a dwarf and everyone is bigger than you. But do you know what Marine Corps training is designed to do?"

"Yeah," Woody answered. "It teaches you how to fight and all that stuff."

Paula shook her head. "No, learning how to fight and how to shoot is easy. And it does give you confidence. The real lesson of Marine Corps training is you are capable of doing a lot more than you think you can. What limits most people, what causes most failures, what makes most people lose, is they simply give up. They don't think they can do anything more. What the Marine Corps taught me was, *yes, you can*."

"What happens when you do everything you can, but you still lose?" Terry asked angrily. "I'm a dwarf. There is only so much I can do."

"Wait here," Paula commanded. She left the room.

"What is she up to?" Woody inquired.

Terry simply shrugged his shoulders.

Paula returned with a young girl. "Terry, Woody, I would like you to meet Cathy, who is fourteen and weighs less than one hundred pounds."

"Nice to meet you," Terry said extending his hand.

"Likewise," Woody responded with a wave.

Paula pointed to Woody. "You look like you can take care of yourself."

"Should be. I used to be a boxer before I became a cab driver." Woody danced around a bit and threw a few punches in the air.

"Were you any good?"

"I won more than I lost. I managed to win a Golden Gloves title."

"Great," Paula said clapping her hands together. "Then you will have no trouble with fighting Cathy."

"I'm not going to fight some kid. I'll kill her."

"No, you won't," Cathy answered with a grin. "But I promise I won't hurt you."

"Are you serious?" Woody asked.

"Absolutely," answered Cathy.

Paula went over and pulled Woody by the arm to the center of the room. "Look you don't have to kill her. Just spar with her. Try to hit her. It's okay if you pull your punches." Paula faced Cathy. "I expect you to go easy on him."

Cathy smiled. She approached Woody, stopping about four feet in front of him. Woody reluctantly put up his hands. At first, he gently tried to slap her. Each time Cindy easily avoided the blow. Woody noticed she was light on her feet, never really standing still.

"Don't be afraid," Paula yelled from the wall she was leaning against. "You're not going to hurt her."

Woody decided to give her the *old one, two*. He jabbed with his left and followed through with his right. Cathy grabbed hold of Woody's right wrist, at the same time turning on her feet to where she was outside of Woody's right side, with her back against his. Still holding onto his wrist, she stepped back with her left foot, forcing Woody to lose his balance. She pushed Woody's arm with her free hand, sending him to the floor, flat on his back. She then pulled on his arm and forced him on his stomach. Her final move was to place a wrist lock on him.

"Hey that hurts," Woody yelled.

Cathy let go of his arm and jumped up.

Woody took a bit longer to get to his feet.

"Don't stop," Cathy said egging him on.

Woody started bouncing around on the balls of his feet, like he used to when he was boxing. He started circling the young girl. He jumped forward and jabbed with his left. Cathy blocked the blow with her left arm, giving her the opportunity to twirl around inside of Woody's reach and bringing her right elbow into his ribs. Woody was stunned by the attack which gave Cathy enough time to reach down, grabbed both of his legs, and pull up. Again, Woody ended up on the floor. Cathy bounced away to face Woody.

"That's enough," Paula said. "I think you proved my point."

"What's that?" Woody ask as he got up from the floor.

"The point is it's not size, or strength, that wins," Paula replied. "It's cunning, skills, confidence, and most of all, not giving up. Also, you underestimated her."

"But I'll bet she's had years of training," Terry interjected. "I can't spend years learning to defend myself. I need to know how to do it now."

"Don't worry," said Paula. "What I'm going to teach you doesn't require years of training. You just need to learn a few tricks and not to give up."

~ ~ ~

Woody enjoyed the two hours of exercise with Paula and Terry. It wasn't anything like what he had done when he was boxing, but it did give him a chance to vent some of his anger and frustration. He thought it was funny the way Paula had easily thwarted Terry's attacks. But as time went on, Terry caught on, and Woody became impressed with how the little guy held up.

"Don't stop," Paula yelled at Terry as he practiced overcoming Cathy. "Don't stop until you have completely incapacitated your opponent. You don't want him to get back up. You want to break his bones, knock him unconscious, kill him if you have to. But *never, never*, give him the opportunity to get back up."

"Damn, you're vicious, woman," Woody said with a small laugh.

Paula stared at Woody. "When you boxed, it was a sport with rules. On the street, it's life or death, and there are no rules. I'm a firm believer you should walk away from a fight whenever you can. Don't let your ego get you into trouble. You should never start a fight. But if you find yourself in one, make damn sure you finish it; and you do that by beating the crap out of your opponent. There is no such thing as a fair fight in the streets."

Cathy jumped up. "He's getting pretty good at this."

"I wish," Terry said as he got up off the mat. "It's easy to take you down. You're cooperating. You're letting me win. That's not going to happen in real life."

"No, it's not," Paula replied. "Use your secret weapon to your advantage. Your size makes others think they can easily defeat you. When you fight back, you surprise them, and you can use that surprise to defeat them. They will underestimate you and their overconfidence gives you an advantage, so use it."

~ ~ ~

Marshall slammed his fist on his desk and jumped up from his chair. "Damn it."

"Okay," Freedman said slowly. "What's wrong now?"

"Those idiots left the stakeout at William Dunn's House."

"Why would they do that?" Freedman asked.

"A kid came up to them and reported seeing Dunn at a

supermarket a few blocks away. They went to check it out, and of course, nothing. But when they returned ten minutes later, they checked the house and garage and noticed the garage was empty. Which means Dunn came back and got whatever was in there, probably his pickup truck with a bullet hole in the tailgate and left."

"So, what do you want to do now?"

Marshall smacked his chair before sitting down. "Well Dunn knows we are staking out his place, so I doubt he'll go back."

Freedman groaned as he got up from his desk and reached for his coffee cup. "So, let's pull the stakeout team. No need to waste manpower. I'll make some more coffee. I got a feeling it's going to be a long night."

Marshall reached for the phone on his desk. "And I've got to call home to tell them I'm working late, again."

~ ~ ~

"To go or not to go," Diana said to herself as she walked to the door of Murphy's, "Twis it nobler to go for a drink or to go home, and perhaps to sleep..."

"It's better you say nothing," a voice interrupted her parody of Hamlet's famous soliloquy. A hand clasped over Diana's face before she could turn to see who was talking to her. She struggled to free herself, only to lose consciousness.

For a few seconds, Billy stood there, making sure Diana unconscious. He removed the rag soaked in ether. He didn't know how long she would remain unconscious. He put her arm over his shoulder and his free arm around her waist. He half carried and half dragged her to his pickup and placed her in the passenger seat. For extra good measure, Billy put the ether-soaked cloth over Diana's face as he went around to the driver's side.

~ ~ ~

Working in a bar gave Becky several things. One was money to pay the rent. Two was a chance to meet some very interesting people. Three was a sense of when something was not right. It was number three that caught her attention as she parked her car. Becky recognized Diana, but not the man who seemed to be dragging her to a pickup truck with lots of dents in its side. Diana looked drunk, very drunk. Becky took out her cell phone. She knew better than to chase trouble, but there was nothing wrong with getting a picture of the truck and hopefully a clear shot of the man. Becky took a deep breath. She was reluctant to call the police because she would hate to bother them if it turned out to be nothing. But there was a nagging feeling deep inside screaming for her to call the police. By the time she entered Murphy's she had made up her mind.

~ ~ ~

Terry was grateful. Paula finally finished the lesson and the abuse of his body. Terry felt like a basketball from the way Cathy had thrown him around. Right now, Terry just wanted a beer and an ice pack for his body.

"Hey, not a bad place," Woody said as they entered Murphy's. "How did you find this place?"

"A lot of journalists hang out here," Terry answered. "Also, it's not far from where I work."

Becky noticed the large black man first, then she saw Terry. They were making their way through the crowd, looking for a table when Becky ran up to them.

"Good, I found you," she said breathlessly. "I think something bad has happened."

"What?" Terry asked.

Becky took a deep breath. "Earlier, I saw someone take Diana away in his car."

"Okay," Terry said slowly.

"You don't understand," Becky continued. "Something didn't seem right. I think he somehow drugged her. I called the police. A patrol unit came by and took a report. They said they would notify other units to look for the vehicle, but

I haven't heard anything back from them yet, and it's been at least two hours."

"What kind of car did the guy have," Woody asked as he surveyed the room, still looking for a table.

"A blue pickup, with a lot of dents in its side," Becky answered.

Terry grabbed his phone from his pocket and hit speed dial, calling Diana. "Come on, come on; answer the phone."

Becky and Woody watched Terry as he began to pace around. They could hear the phone ringing. It stopped. Someone answered.

A man's voice came over the phone. "Hello Terry,"

Becky could see the fear in Terry's face. "Where is Diana?" Terry demanded.

"Why, she's with me."

"Billy, you listen to me..."

"No, you listen to me," Billy shouted interrupting Terry. "You sent the police to my house. You couldn't just do your part. Well now, the game has changed."

Terry's hand was shaking. "What do you want?"

"You!"

Becky kept shaking her head no. Woody put his hand on her shoulder. "Don't worry little lady. I'll be with him."

Becky looked up to Woody. "No offense, but who are you? Are you a cop or something?"

Terry shushed them both by holding up his hand. "I want to talk to Diana."

"You don't get to make demands," Billy answered. "You need to be at the shopping center where you found the first body at ten o'clock. That's in two hours. If you're not there, then your friend is going to learn a new definition of pain. And come alone. If there is anyone else, you and your friend get it."

"If you hurt her..."

"You'll do what? Listen shrimp. Be at the shopping center,

alone, or else your friend suffers." The call ended.

Terry punched recall. The phone rang, but there was no response. Finally, Terry turned his phone off and put it back in his pocket.

"What are you going to do?" Woody asked. "If you want to go after this guy, count me in."

"You don't know this guy," Terry said. "He's dangerous. He's a killer. I can't take you with me. He told me to come alone or else he will kill Diana."

Woody jabbed his finger at Terry. "No, you don't understand. This son of a bitch killed my sister. I want him to pay for what he did. I want to see him fry in the electric chair."

"I don't think they do that anymore, oh, who cares," Becky interjected. "Now, both of you calm down. You need to call the police. Even if you do show up, he's going to kill you and Diana. He can't have any witnesses. The only chance you have is to call the police."

"No, I have to go alone."

Woody chuckled.

"What's so funny," Terry demanded.

"How are you going to get there?" Woody said smiling. "You don't drive."

"I'll..."

"take a taxi," Woody answered holding up his keys. "Remember, I'm a taxi driver. This way it looks like you are going alone, but I'll be there to watch your back."

"It's still too dangerous," Becky objected. "You need to call the police."

"No, we don't," Woody said forcefully. "What we need to do is get this guy. And we will."

~ ~ ~

Paula exhaled in relief as she sat down in the one easy chair in her apartment. In her left hand was a half-filled glass of whiskey. In her right was the TV remote. She pressed the button to turn on the television. Her phone rang.

She pressed the TV remote again to silence it before picking up her phone.

"This had better be important."

"Is that how you answer your phone?"

"A better question is who is this?"

"It's me Becky. You know, the waitress at Murphy's. *Your friend.*"

Paula leaned forward and set her glass down on the coffee table. "Okay Becky, so what's up? Why are you calling? By the way, how did you get this number?"

"That's not important. What is important is your killer has Diana, and he is demanding Terry to meet with him."

"What? How do you know this?"

"When I came to work, I saw someone take Diana. A few minutes ago, Terry came in with some big, black guy. When I told him what I saw, he tried to call Diana. Someone else answered and he demanded Terry meet him. He told Terry to come alone or else he would kill Diana."

"Do you know where?"

"Some shopping center; that all I could catch."

"When are they supposed to meet?"

"At ten o'clock tonight."

"Where's Terry now?"

"I don't know," Becky answered. "The big guy and Terry left here a few minutes ago. They took off before I could stop them. They think they're cavalry charging in to save Diana."

"And you don't know where."

"All I know is the guy holding Diana told Terry to meet him where he found the first body. I think the killer is talking about where the first murder took place."

"Damn."

"Please," Becky pleaded. "Do something. Terry's in danger."

"Okay. Calm down. I'll take care of it."

"Do you want me to call the police? Terry told me not to.

He's afraid if the police show up, this guy will kill Diana. But I know he's going to kill her and Terry anyway."

"You're right about that," Paula said as she set her drink down on the kitchen counter and walked to her closet. She pulled out her nine-millimeter automatic from a box on the shelf. She made sure to take the two extra magazines and box of shells. "I'll call the police. I know the detective handling the case and I'll make sure he slips in quietly. Right now, don't do anything. You're at work, right?"

"Yes."

"Good. Stay there until you hear from me. You're safe as long as you're in a crowd."

"You don't think the killer's after me, do you?"

"No idea," Paula answered. "But I want to be sure you are safe, so stay at work. Okay?"

"Okay," Becky answered meekly. "What are you going to do?"

"Looks like I get to be the cavalry."

Paula hung up and checked her weapon. The magazine was loaded. She loaded the two extra magazines, then dumped the rest of the nine-millimeter shells in her pocket. They were bulky, but she felt better having the extra ammunition with her. She went to the foot locker that served as her coffee table. She rummaged through the uniforms stored in there until she found a large folding knife, which she stuck in her back pocket. She saw her old dog tags. Failure was not an option, but just in case, she wanted the police to be able to identify her. She slipped the dog tags into her other back pocket. She grabbed a flashlight on her way out the door.

Paula stopped and looked at the damaged driver's side of her car before getting in. She dialed Detective Marshall's number and set the phone on speaker. While the phone was ringing, she started the engine. She was out of the parking lot and on her way when Marshall answered.

Paula didn't give Marshall a chance to speak. "Detective, this is Paula Stanford. I need to know where the first murder occurred. I think Terry is in danger."

"I think you need to explain yourself," Marshall replied.

"I just got a call from a waitress who saw Diana Hawley, a reporter who works with Terry, being kidnapped. According to her, the killer called Terry and told him to meet him at the first murder site..."

"Crap!"

"What's wrong," Paula demanded.

"We got a call about someone being kidnapped a couple of hours ago. It was from a bar waitress. Figures it would be connected to this case. So, our kidnapper is our killer, who called Terry and told Terry to meet him, the killer, at the first murder site."

"That's right."

"The problem is we don't know where the first murder occurred. We found the body behind an abandon shopping center on Highway 41."

"That's got to be it. How soon can you get there?"

"I can have units there in about five minutes..."

"No," Paula screamed. "The killer also told Terry to come alone. If the killer sees anyone, he'll probably kill both Terry and Diana before we can stop it."

Paula could hear Marshall groan. "Then what do you want me to do?" he asked.

"Let me go in. I'll park far enough away so he won't see my car. I think I can get in close enough without being seen. In the meantime, you can try to block off any escape routes. But please don't attract attention. We don't want to spook him."

"Absolutely not," Marshall answered. "This is police business. I need you to stay out of it. If you get hurt, I'll never hear the end of it."

"What did you say? You're breaking up."

"Stanford!!" Marshall yelled through the phone. "I know you can hear me. Stay out of it."

"Sorry, didn't catch what you said. Hanging up. Goodbye."

Paula smiled as she sped towards the scheduled rendezvous between Terry and the killer. Meanwhile Marshall was rushing out the door, calling his partner, and hoping he wouldn't be too late.

Chapter Twenty-Three

Billy was outside the passenger door of the pickup, chuckling as he watched Diana struggle against the duct tape binding her hands behind her. He was quite pleased with himself. He had the foresight to bring duct tape to restrain Diana and to cover her mouth. Billy kept watch on both Diana and the back of the shopping center. He felt it was fitting his last two victims would be found in the same spot as his first one. From the hill they were on, he would see if anyone followed Terry. He also made it a point to be here before anyone else. This way he could see if someone came early and decided to hide, hoping to catch him. Billy wasn't going to allow that. No, he was going to his finish his final kills.

Billy walked over to the truck and smiled at Diana. He could see the fear in her eyes. He opened the door and gently reached up to Diana's ears. He removed her earrings.

Movement caught his eye. It was a car, moving slowly, with its lights off. Could it be Terry? He was more than an hour early. Billy, quickly put the earrings in his pocket. If it was Terry, he was probably hoping to set a trap. Billy looked at the vehicle through his binoculars. He smiled. How appropriate. Terry had come the same way he had first arrived at the scene those weeks ago, in a taxi.

~ ~ ~

"We're too early," Terry said to Woody.

"Relax," Woody replied. "All I have to do is find a

place to hide. When the killer shows up, then we got him."

"Where can you hide behind an abandon shopping center? It's wide open back here."

"Yeah, you're right. I guess I'll have to park down the road and hoof it back here. You going to be okay with me leaving you here for a while?"

"Probably not," Terry answered. "Still what choice do I have?" Terry got out of the cab and watched the taillights as they disappeared around the corner of the building.

~ ~ ~

It didn't feel right to Billy. Yes, the taxi dropped Terry off. Billy could tell it was Terry by his size. But what kind of taxi driver would leave a customer alone in the middle of nowhere? And, why was Terry so early? No, something was not right.

~ ~ ~

The revelation came to Diana as soon as he removed her earrings. This was Billy, the same killer that had taunted Terry and the police these past few weeks. She knew she had to do something, or she would die, here, on this hill. Diana noticed her kidnapper's attention was on the shopping center below the hill. She still couldn't free her hands, but he hadn't taped her feet, so if she could get out without him noticing, then she could run. Diana quietly stepped out of the pickup. She managed to get her feet on the ground. She took a step and slipped, causing the door to close. In the still night air, the sound was deafening.

~ ~ ~

Billy heard the door close. He turned to see Diana standing there, her hands still bound behind her and tape over her mouth. He watched as she stared back at him. She started to run. Billy was amused until he realized she was running downhill, towards Terry. Billy started to run after her. Then he realized, this was exactly what he wanted: both Terry and Diana behind the shopping center. He returned to his truck and started the engine.

~ ~ ~

Terry heard footsteps, awkward footsteps. *Woody sounds like a wounded elephant* Terry thought as he searched for the source of the footsteps. It sounded like the someone falling in the brush at the edge of the pavement behind the shopping center. There were grunts and the sounds of someone moving through the brush. Slowly, a figure came into the light. He could see it was Diana. She was running with her hands behind her back. Terry ran towards her.

"Diana," he exclaimed as he reached her. Seeing the tape on Diana's mouth, Terry reached up and gently pulled it off.

"It's a trap," Diana yelled. "You have to get out of here. The killer's here, and he's going to kill us."

"I'm not leaving you," Terry said as he went around Diana's back to free her hands. "Where did you last see him?"

The bright lights of a pickup truck illuminated the area as it pulled up and stopped less than twenty feet from Terry and Diana. From behind the lights came a laugh. "Why, I'm right here."

With Diana's hands freed, they both faced the lights. Terry put up his hand to shield his eyes. "You don't have to do this Billy. The police know who you are. It's only a matter of time before they catch you. Killing us won't make any difference."

Billy laughed harder. "You're right about it not making any difference; so why not kill you? Imagine the satisfaction I will get from it. Seeing you two grovel for your lives. Really, Terry, to think, we had a good thing going. I would call you and you would get a news story. All you had to do was answer the phone. But no, you brought others into it. You made it harder for me to continue. Don't you see Terry. This is all your fault. All you had to do was answer the phone."

Terry stepped in front of Diana. "If your beef is with me, then let Diana go. She didn't have anything to do with it."

Billy stepped into the light. "Nice try *shrimp*; but I'm afraid you both have to die."

~ ~ ~

Boy, am I out of shape Woody thought as he jogged back to the shopping center. He was breathing hard and had to stop several times to catch his breath. He was still breathing heavily when he came around the corner and saw a man standing in front of a pickup, pointing a gun at Terry and some lady.

He was glad the truck was running. The sound of the engine would cover his footsteps if he was careful. He wanted to circle around and come up behind the truck and surprise the man with the gun. Woody made it to the back of the truck. He took a quick look in the bed of the truck to see if he could find something to use as a weapon. He was in luck. There was a tool box. He slowly opened the box, quietly searched in the limited light for a screwdriver. He found one. He picked it up. It got caught on the hammer, which fell out of the tool box.

~ ~ ~

Billy smiled as he leveled his gun at Terry. Then he heard a noise. Billy turned to see a large dark shape coming at him. Billy quickly realized a man was attacking him. He turned and pointed his gun at the shape, firing twice.

~ ~ ~

"Run," Terry screamed as he ran towards Billy. He thrust out his arms, hitting Billy's arm and torso,

shoving him into the headlights of the truck. Terry kicked at Billy's knee, bringing Billy to the ground where Terry kicked him several times. Terry grabbed Billy's head and started banging it against the front of the truck.

Diana ran up to Terry, grabbed his arm, and pulled him away. "Let's go," she demanded, dragging him behind her as she ran behind the truck.

Billy groaned. It took him almost a minute before he was able to stand up. He went to the cab of the pickup, stopping only to look at the large man lying on the ground. He jumped into the cab, put the truck into gear and backed up. He started after his two fleeing victims. They would not escape.

~ ~ ~

Paula heard the shots. *Forget stealth*, she thought, *it's now time for action.* Her tires squealed as Paula speed around the corner of the shopping center, with her high beams on to give her more light. Speed was her ally. Paula saw two shadows running and headlights chasing them. She pressed the gas pedal, heading to intercept the vehicle chasing the two people. The driver of the other vehicle must have seen her headlights, but he continued towards his targets, increasing his speed. Paula cursed under her breath as she ran her car into the front of the truck, forcing it to lose a wheel and come to a grinding halt. The airbag in the steering wheel exploded into her chest, knocking the breath out of her. Her car was a wreck, but she was okay.

Paula took a couple of deep breaths, grabbed her pistol, and jumped out of her car. "Freeze you son of a bitch. Move one inch and I'll shoot," she shouted as she leveled her weapon at the cab of the truck.

Paula waited for a response. None came. She slowly edged her way around her car, continuously keeping her weapon focused on the cab of the pickup truck. She paused at the rear of her car, pistol pointed where the driver should be. She took a careful look around. The shadows provided too many hiding places.

"You okay?" said a voice startling Paula. She jumped back behind her car and turn to face her new assailant.

"Hey, be careful of where you point that thing," said a shadow. It moved into the light, and Paula could see it was Terry. Behind him, crouched low was Diana.

Paula pointed to a spot by the rear fender. "You two stay here. Don't move. I'll see if I can find our killer."

"No, don't go," Diana pleaded. "It's too dangerous. He has a gun, and I know he wants to kill us and anyone who gets in the way."

Paula glared at Diana. "What do you think I'm holding, a pickle?"

Paula turned to face the pickup. She smiled when she heard the sirens, faintly in the distance, knowing help would soon be there. She only had to keep him here till the police arrived.

~ ~ ~

Billy heard the sirens in the distance. He knew he had to get out of there. *But who ran into him?* Then he saw her. It was that tall blonde, the one who had been chasing him because of a minor fender bender at the fairgrounds parking lot. He could tell she had a pistol, and that it was pointed at him. He took a breath and thought about jumping out and having a good old-fashion shootout. But he had seen her shoot. He knew a shootout would end badly for him.

But she stopped. She went back to the other side of her car. Then he saw she was talking to Terry and Diana, who had come back to help her. This was his chance. While she was busy with them, he managed to crawl out of the window on the passenger side. The shadows hid him as he made his way back to the brush at the outer edge of the pavement.

Billy heard the large man he had shot groan. Billy got down on one knee and looked into the blackness. He saw nothing, which gave him hope that no one else could see him either.

~ ~ ~

Damn, getting shot really hurts, Woody thought as he laid on the pavement. He tried moving, but even sitting up hurt. He was grateful the guy who shot him drove off. He was fearful the same guy would return and finish what he had started.

When the car crashed into the pickup, Woody willed himself to fight the pain and drag himself to safety. The only place he could think of was the brush at the edge of the pavement. It was about thirty feet away. He had managed to drag himself less than ten feet when he saw someone sneaking across the pavement. Woody stopped, hoping the other individual wouldn't see him. Woody heard sirens coming closer, but they were still in the distance. Then he saw another figure, this one cautiously approaching the truck.

Woody realized the shadow halfway across the pavement was the person who shot him; the person who had killed his sister. Woody didn't want him to get away. He took a deep breath. "Hey. Look out. The killer is over here."

~ ~ ~

Billy turned to face the person who yelled. *Why can't you be quiet?* Billy didn't want to say anything aloud to avoid giving away his position. He took a quick look behind him and saw a figure moving towards him. He had to decide who to shoot. He pointed his pistol at the shadow coming after him and pulled the trigger twice.

~ ~ ~

Being shot at was not a new experience for Paula. She saw movement ahead and knew to hit the deck. She heard the bullets pass by.

~ ~ ~

Terry saw Paula dive to the ground. He didn't know why, but he knew he should also get down, but not before making sure Diana was safe. What possessed him, he'll never know. Terry ran and tackled Diana to the ground, just before two bullets hit Paula's car.

~ ~ ~

Billy didn't wait to see if he managed to hit anyone. He ran.

~ ~ ~

"Stay down," Paula yelled from her position on the ground. She raised her head to see if Billy was still shooting at them. Paula saw a shape running. She knew it was Billy. She got up and started to run after him.

She hadn't covered more than few yards when she heard someone call for help. She stopped and followed the moans.

"Hey big guy, I've got you," Paula said as she knelt down to help Woody. "Where are you hit?"

"Forget me," Woody insisted. "Go after that son of a bitch. Get him."

Paula placed her pistol in the waistband behind her back. "We'll have plenty of time for that," she said. She pulled out her phone and dialed 9-1-1 calling for an ambulance.

~ ~ ~

Billy reached the brush standing at the edge of the pavement. He pushed through the brush. He stopped after a few minutes and turned. He saw no one was following. He was able to make out a person kneeling on the ground, probably helping the man he had shot. He smiled, realizing he was escaping. Billy turned and continued his way to freedom. He also vowed this was not over.

~ ~ ~

Three patrol cars pulled up, each one focusing its headlights on different areas behind the shopping center. Marshall and Freedman got out of an unmarked vehicle and spotted Terry as he got off of Diana, who was lying on the ground.

"Are you okay?" Marshall asked, rushing over to Terry and Diana.

"Yeah, yeah, we're okay," answered Terry. "But I think Woody was shot."

"Hey," they heard Paula calling. "We need an ambulance."

Everyone came running over. One of the patrol officers realized Woody was wounded and he called on his radio for an ambulance.

"Where's Billy," Marshall demanded.

Terry and Diana noticed Paula wasn't there. Terry pointed to the brush about twenty feet away. "I think Billy ran into there. I bet Paula went after him."

"Great," Marshall screamed, "that's all we need. Another civilian to get shot."

Freedman pulled out his cell phone. "I'm calling in K-9. We'll let the dogs track him. In the meantime, let's send a couple of units up to the top of the hill over there and hope we can trap him."

Four officers ran back to their patrol vehicles and took off.

~ ~ ~

Billy was out of breath by the time he made to the top of the hill. He looked down the small slope, seeing two patrol vehicles leaving the scene. He knew they were coming to get him. He turned and ran down the road. He managed to get about two hundred yards down the road when he saw flashes of light from the patrol vehicles. He jumped into a ditch and watched the patrol cars speed by. Billy got back up and continued running away from the scene.

~ ~ ~

What's taking the ambulance so long thought Terry. "Don't worry," Terry said as he patted Woody on the shoulder.

"No problem," Woody replied. "I've had worse from when I was in the ring. Don't worry about me. Go get the killer. Don't let him get away."

"He won't," said Marshall as he directed Freedman to position their vehicle with its headlights on the brush behind the shopping center. Marshall had the remaining patrol car position its headlights on Woody and keep it's flashing lights on to make it easier for the ambulance to find them. "I've got Freedman putting out a BOLO, a 'be on the lookout' for Billy. We've got every available unit, including K-9, responding to this location. It's only a matter of time before we get him.

~ ~ ~

Paula knelt down to listen for movement. Combat had taught her to use all of her senses. She remembered what one instructor had said. "To survive in combat, you need to listen to grass grow." She heard movement to her right. Then came the patrol vehicles with their lights. Paula closed her eyes. She didn't want to lose her night vision. She knew looking into the lights would cause the pupils of her eyes to contract, making it more difficult to see in the dark. The vehicles passed. She continued to listen. She heard the footsteps on the pavement.

~ ~ ~

Billy kept running. He knew he had to get a car quickly. He stopped and bent over with his hands on his knees to catch his breath. He heard something. He stood up and listened. Yes, he heard something.

Someone was running after him.

~ ~ ~

Paula had no trouble closing the distance between them. But the steps stopped. She could no longer hear them. She knew Billy had heard her. He was somewhere ahead, waiting for her, waiting to kill her.

~ ~ ~

The footsteps stopped. Billy knew whoever was chasing him would not stop. He simply had to be quiet until that person came to him.

~ ~ ~

Paula cautiously moved forward, staying in the shadows as much as possible. This was a dangerous game, looking for an enemy hiding and waiting to ambush you. He had the advantage. It didn't matter. She was not going to let him get away.

~ ~ ~

The ambulance arrived along with another patrol unit and two K-9 units. The paramedics started preparing Woody for transporting to the hospital while the K-9 units were getting briefed by Freedman.

Marshall pulled Terry and Diana aside. "I need you two to go with the guy who got shot. I need you out of the area. I've got K-9 here and we're going in after Billy. But I have to get you two to safety."

"What about Paula?" Diana asked. "She's out there chasing the killer. What's going to happen to her?"

"When I find that blond Amazon, I'm going to shoot her," an annoyed Marshall replied. "Marine training or not, she knows better to go after a killer in the brush at night. We'll be lucky if we find her alive."

"But she's a Marine. She's been trained for this.," Terry stressed.

"You're wrong," Marshall said as he checked his weapon. "She was trained for combat with other Marines backing her up. *We've* been trained for this, and furthermore, *we've* handled situations like this before. This is nothing new for us."

Diana reached out and touched Marshall's arm. "Bring Paula back safely; and get that son of a bitch."

"We'll get him," Marshall said as he turned to join the other officers preparing to enter the brush.

~ ~ ~

Paula slowly continued forward. She stopped and smiled. She heard the K-9 units and officers as they began to move through the brush. Her enemy lost his advantage.

~ ~ ~

Billy heard the dog barking. He knew what it meant. He got up from his hidden position; but stopped. He saw a form in the shadows. He knelt back down and waited. A minute later he saw the form again, this time closer to him. Billy smiled. It was that tall blond, the one who kept chasing after him. Well, if she wanted him to find him that badly, the least he could do was oblige her.

Billy waited till she was less than twenty feet away. He carefully aimed his pistol. He pulled the trigger.

~ ~ ~

Marshall heard the shot. So, did the dogs and the others in the search party. "Keep the dogs quiet," Marshall demanded. He listened, hoping for some other sounds. There were none. Marshall held up his fist. "Everyone, move forward, quietly. Our killer is out there waiting for us."

~ ~ ~

A sixth sense made Paula stop and drop down to her knees. The bullet struck a tree behind her. She threw herself to the ground, crawling to find any cover she could.

"Don't move," Billy demanded. "I've got you covered."

Paula stayed flat, silently moving her weapon in the direction of the voice. "Do you hear that?" she yelled back. "That's the police with K-9 units. It's only a matter of minutes before they get here. Be smart. Give yourself up."

"No," Billy said quietly, but forcefully. "I've got you in my sights. Now put your gun on the ground and slide it over to me."

Paula hesitated.

"I said put your weapon on the ground and slide it over to me."

"Okay," Paula yelled. She placed her nine-millimeter on the pavement and slid over until it was about three feet beyond her reach. "Here it is."

Billy came out of his hiding place. He walked over and kicked Paula's automatic further away from her. "Now get up, and no funny business."

Paula got to her feet. "Now what are you going to do?" She made sure to talk in a loud voice.

Billy smiled. "Haven't really thought about it; but I'm sure I'll come up with something."

Paula nodded towards the noise. "They're getting closer. You don't have much time."

"Don't you worry about it," Billy said. "I've enough time to put a couple of bullets into you."

"Yeah, you do," Paula loudly acknowledge. "Then what. Don't you understand? In a few minutes you will be in police custody or dead."

"And you care so much about my personal welfare," Billy responded in a sarcastic voice.

Paula threw her hands up and dropped them to her side. "Me, not really," she said forcefully. "Whether you come out of this dead or alive doesn't make a damn bit of difference to me. So, you choose." Paula put her hands into her back pockets. She felt the knife in her hand.

"Well, before I kill you, perhaps you can answer a question for me."

"Sure Billy. What is it?"

"Why did you come after me? I know why Terry did. I called him. I made him part of the game. But you. You chased after me because of a broken headlight. What made you so vengeful?"

Paula smiled. "I'll admit I was pissed about you smashing my headlight and fender. But when you killed Kelly, it became much more important than a smashed fender."

"Kelly? Who's Kelly?"

"The young lady you killed at my gym," Paula answered in an angry and loud voice. "She was the receptionist. She was a college student, working on a business degree. You stole her dreams, her ambitions, her life. And, what about the others? Why kill them?"

Billy chuckled. "Well, you'll never know bitch. Take those questions to the grave with you." Billy raised his pistol and took aim.

"If that's the way you want it," Paula said. She turned on the ball of her left foot 270 degrees and threw the knife at Billy just as he pulled the trigger.

~ ~ ~

Marshall heard the voices. He grinned as he signaled for the K-9 units to keep the dogs quiet. He listened again. It was that Marine, shouting, directing them to where Billy was. Marshall motioned for everyone to move forward, again cautioning them to be quiet. Then he heard another shot. Marshall turned to the K-9 units. "Let the dogs go."

~ ~ ~

The bullet missed Paula, as did her knife miss Billy. Billy dropped to the ground, and this gave Paula enough time to attack. Billy brought his pistol up to shoot. Paula grabbed his hand and forced the barrel of the weapon away from her. Instead of trying to take the weapon away, Paula kicked with her right foot, first kicking Billy in the knee, then in the balls. Billy dropped the pistol when he fell to the ground. Paula kicked the pistol away. She saw her knife a few feet away. She lunged for it, grabbed it, and brought it down in Billy's shoulder. She pulled it out, lifting it high above her head.

Something gripped her hand. Paula turned to see a dog holding onto her arm. Billy laughed and reached for the gun he had dropped. Another dog ran forward and latched onto his arm. The animal started dragging Billy away from the weapon. Paula stopped struggling. The dog held on, but its bite wasn't as strong.

Police officers came up and put leashes on the dogs. They gave the dogs a command and they let Paula and Billy go. Paula was surprised the dog's bite barely penetrated the skin of her arm. Billy was not so lucky. Paula could see blood dripping from his arm.

Paula slowly stood up and turned to see Marshall, along with several other police officers. "What took you so damn long?"

Chapter Twenty-Four

Fitch has seen many things in his thirty years as a newspaper reporter and editor. He didn't know what to make of it seeing a tall blond with a bandage on one arm and a pistol in her lap, asleep in a chair at the copy editor's desk. He slowly started to get back on the elevator.

"Hey, good morning," Terry said as he walked back to his desk with a cup of coffee. "You're in early."

Fitch put his finger to his lips to quiet Terry. He pointed to the tall blond. Terry looked over to where he was pointing.

"He's freaked out about me," a sleepy Paula said as she sat up. "Guess he's not used to seeing someone with a weapon sleeping in his office."

Terry smiled and gestured to Paula. "Oh, that's Paula Stanford. She's a friend of mine. She helped us catch the killer."

"Have they caught him?" Fitch asked rushing forward.

"Yes," Paula answered as she stretched and yawned.

"Details," Fitch demanded.

Paula stood up and stretched again. "Terry, you fill him in on the details. I'm going home to get some sleep."

"No, you're not," Diana stated with determination as she walked into the office. Becky was with her. "I'm going to take you, along with Becky here, to breakfast for saving our lives." Diana walked over to Terry and gave him a hug and a kiss on the cheek. "And that's for saving my life. You're a real hero."

"Who's this," Fitch demanded pointing to Becky.

"A friend," Paula answered.

"Oh, how sweet," Becky responded. She went over and gave Paula a hug. "And yes, I am your friend."

"She's also your new reporter," Diana stated.

Fitch gave Diana a confused look. "My new reporter? I should hire her?"

"Yes, you should," Paula answered. "This is Ms. Becky Watson. Yes, she's a bit strange, but she's a brilliant young scholar who will amaze you with her insight."

Again, Fitch looked confused.

"She's smart and you're going to love having her work here," Diana added.

Fitch resigned to the fact he now had a new reporter. But he faced Diana. "So, just where were you last night?"

"I spent half the night being tied up in a pickup truck with a killer, and the other half at home taking a very long shower." Diana turned to Terry, "How is the guy who got shot?"

"Good news," Terry answered. "I stopped by the hospital on the way in. The bullets missed any vital organs. The doctors said he'll be in the hospital for about a week, and it will take him a while to fully recover; but he's going to be fine."

Paula groaned as she sat back down. "Why can't I go home and take a shower? Oh, wait. I know why. I don't have a car."

"Well I have some good news about that," Terry said. He pulled out a set of car keys. "Woody asked me to look after his taxi while he's in the hospital. I'm sure he won't mind you using it until he gets back on his feet."

"Great," Paula gleefully exclaimed. "Where is it?"

"Uh, I don't know," Terry sheepishly answered.

"Well it's a good thing we know."

Everyone turned to see Marshall and Steven standing by the elevator. "It turns out your friend left his taxi about half a mile from the shopping center we were at last night."

Marshall pointed to Paula. "By the way, I had your car towed to our impound lot last night. It looks like a total loss."

"Yeah, well, I'll get over it," Paula replied. "What about the piece of garbage I stabbed last night? Is he going to live?"

"Yeah," Marshall answered.

"You should have let me finish the job," Paula said with a degree of anger in her voice. "It would have saved the state some money."

"Actually, I'm glad you didn't," Marshall said as he sat down.

"Has he confessed?" Diana asked.

"Are you kidding," Steven answered with a chuckle. "This guy couldn't wait to make a deal with the district attorney. They took the death penalty off the table. The way this guy is singing, you would think he's trying out for *American Idol*. We can't shut him up."

Terry opened his desk drawer and looked at the photo of Kristen. "So why did he do it? Was it just to get his name in the papers?"

"Not quite," Marshall replied. "The first victim, Frances Colton, was his girlfriend. It turns out he was hoping she would help him get a publishing contract through her father, who is some big wig in Hollywood. According to him, he did everything for her; even bought her some expensive diamond earrings."

"And he took them back when he killed her, didn't he," Diana asked.

Marshall nodded in agreement. "It looks that way."

"We got a warrant to search his house," Steven added. "I was over there with some other crime scene techs. We found a whole bunch of earrings. I'm sure with DNA testing, we'll be able to match them with the victims."

"Well, a pair of those earrings are mine," Diana interjected.

Paula took in a heavy breath and sighed. "I wish we had

caught him before he killed Kelly."

"Sorry about your coworker," Marshall said pointing to Paula. "You were right about the victims. They were victims of opportunity except for the first one, the girlfriend. The others, just in the wrong place at the wrong time."

"Thanks, but that doesn't help," Paula acknowledged. "Kelly was a sweet girl. She didn't deserve what happened to her.

Terry's phone rang. He reached to pick it up. He stopped before his hand reached the phone. It continued to ring. "To think it all started because I answered the phone. If I hadn't answered it, if we hadn't given him the publicity he wanted, none of this would have happened."

"No," said Paula. "It would have happened. Billy was a psychopath. He would have killed no matter what."

The phone continued to ring.

"So, what do we do?" Terry asked.

The phone stopped ringing.

"Write the story," Fitch answered. "Write it telling the victims' stories. Take away this killer's glory." Fitch put his hands on Terry's shoulders. "Write the story."

Thank you for reading.

Please review this book. Reviews help others find Absolutely Amazing eBooks and inspire us to keep providing these marvelous tales.

If you would like to be put on our email list to receive updates on new releases, contests, and promotions, please go to AbsolutelyAmazingEbooks.com and sign up.

About the Author

Mark Zeid spent seven and half years as a military police officer for the U.S. Marine Corps. After leaving active duty, he completed an undergraduate degree in literature and graduate studies in English. But the Marines called to him and he reenlisted in the reserves, from which he retired in 2004. Along the way, he spent 25 years living and working in Japan, which included teaching criminal justice for a satellite campus on military bases in the Far East. He also completed graduate study in criminal justice and worked for the Center for Domestic Preparedness, a training facility ran by FEMA that prepares our nation's first responders to deal with mass casualty and terrorists' events. His field experience includes helping several agencies with investigations and community policing, as well as being deployed to assist with disaster recovery efforts in Japan and the United States.

www.ingramcontent.com/pod-product-compliance
Lightning Source LLC
Chambersburg PA
CBHW061438030726
47503CB00005B/1465